BARON OF BAD
LORDS OF SCANDAL

TAMMY ANDRESEN

Copyright © 2022 by Tammy Andresen

All rights reserved.

No part of this book may be reproduced in any form or by any electronic or mechanical means, including information storage and retrieval systems, without written permission from the author, except for the use of brief quotations in a book review.

❦ Created with Vellum

Keep up with all the latest news, sales, freebies, and releases by joining my newsletter!

www.tammyandresen.com

Hugs!

CHAPTER ONE

Lady Grace Chase gripped the side of the carriage with increasingly stiff fingers as she eyed the pale-faced blonde woman who sat across from her.

Lady Cristina Abernath held a long dagger in her thin hand as she stared back at Grace. "It didn't have to be this way."

Grace parted her lips to reply, but hesitated. She wasn't the most sensible woman in England. In fact, of her three sisters and two cousins whom she'd grown up with, she might be the least intelligent of the bunch. But she knew, instinctually, when it was best to keep quiet. And now was one of those times.

Not that she always listened to her instincts. A few hours prior, she'd ignored her feelings entirely and stomped out of the carriage after she'd had a rather heated disagreement with the Baron of Baderness.

He'd accused her of being spoiled and she'd stormed off because of what he'd said, which of course, had allowed her to be kidnapped right in the middle of a busy London Street. If he were here now, she'd smack him, or hug him.

Maybe both.

"If one of your family could have just agreed to help me, I wouldn't have had to take these measures. And then you went and stole my Harry too."

This time, words burned on the tip of Grace's tongue, but she held them in. Accusations like Abernath had chosen to abandon the child in a locked room during a fire or that she'd stolen Grace's sister, Cordelia, and attempted to take her other sister, Diana, recently. Instead, Grace tightened her hold on the wooden rail that trimmed the interior. It was a lovely carriage. She took in the rich red drapery and the shining mahogany of the interior. What an odd prison in which she was now held.

"We can still make a deal. Tell me you're the most rational of the Chase women."

"Hardly," Grace murmured without meaning to. "But I'm willing to talk." Grace was by no means the most rational, which was likely a good thing. Cordelia was far more sensible, for example. But that wouldn't help her in this situation. Abernath was completely off her rocker.

Rather than relaxing, Abernath tensed, narrowing her gaze. "One of your sisters already made that promise. I'm not sure I trust your word."

Grace shrugged, feigning indifference. She was being held at knifepoint in a carriage that was barreling down a country road with a scarred giant of a driver. Blood rushed through her ears. But she was the one who shouldn't be trusted? "I'm sure Diana made you promises. If I'm not mistaken, she likes you." That wasn't entirely true. Diana was the oldest daughter of the Earl of Winthorpe and the boldest of the bunch. She'd likened herself to Abernath, saying that she understood the countess's struggle. Being a strong woman, she'd been trapped into a corner by society.

Abernath, if Grace understood the story correctly, had cheated on her fiancé, the Duke of Darlington. He'd ended the engagement, but the countess had been pregnant and married the Count of Abernath out of necessity.

"Likes me?" Lady Abernath lowered the knife a bit. "I'm not foolish enough to believe that."

Grace swallowed a lump while fisting up her skirts with her free hand. Perhaps she should have stayed silent. While stolen away, she was at least in one piece and she'd prefer to remain that way. She took a long breath. "Diana takes on the world with a strength and fight I could never imagine. Sometimes it's a great asset, other times it makes her life infinitely more difficult. I suppose like is the wrong word. Kinship might be the better choice."

Abernath slumped back against her seat, the dagger dropping to her knee. "That does sound as though it could be true." Her face was frighteningly pale. "Can I tell you something?"

Grace leaned forward. "Of course." Her breath was coming in short gasps and her eyes widened, but she kept her voice calm.

Abernath looked out the window. "I'm dying."

Her confession sent Grace back in her seat. "I beg your pardon?"

"Not even Crusher knows." And she nodded toward the front of the carriage. Grace could only assume he was the frightening driver.

"Are you shivering?" Grace asked, her gaze narrowing.

"Never you mind," Abernath snapped. "Daring owes me for what he did to my life."

The woman was vacillating wildly, which made Grace more afraid than any other part of this experience. Her insides churned with fear as she pressed back into her seat. She held out her hands in front of her, making soft shushing noises. "I understand. He hurt you."

Abernath nodded. Then, amazingly, she set the blade to the side and began pulling off her gloves. Grace sat silently transfixed wondering what might be happening.

The moment the first glove came off, Grace had to gulp down her cry. Abernath's hands were covered in angry welts. "Oh dear," she whispered, not sure what else to say. She looked into the woman's eyes, which were glassy and unfocused. "Do they hurt?"

Slowly Abernath leaned forward, holding herself as she rocked. "Try to understand," she whispered. "They went away and now they've come back." The woman shook like a leaf. "I didn't want to hurt anyone, not you and not your sisters, but men won't help me. Men are the problem not the solution. Even my son—" She stopped. "I've never had female friends, but I need someone to aid me now."

Grace swallowed. "Men are the problem? Sometimes I think I know what you mean." She thought back to her fight with Bad. She didn't understand it at all. First, he wasn't that handsome. His nose was crooked and his skin was craggy. Well, he was dark and mysterious, and there was something powerful in his every movement and gesture, a confidence that seemed to radiate from within. Like he could handle anything.

But truly handsome, he wasn't. And she'd thought that meant she wasn't really interested in his attention. That was to say, she liked almost all attention but it didn't need to be his.

And he'd been attentive, if she were honest. But that was more because his friends had required him to be so. And perhaps that bothered her too. He should be spending time with her because he wanted to. She was attractive. Some even called her beautiful, and she was fun, or she tried to be. But he'd yelled at her today, called her spoiled and selfish and…and she'd give anything to see his hard-dark face right now. Because if he were here, he'd surely make her feel as though everything was all right.

And then she could smack him for making her storm off like that.

"You haven't had a life like mine. I can see it in the sweet expression on your face. Your father, he was kind to you and I bet he didn't take advantage…" Her voice trailed off as she pressed her welted hands together. "Sometimes I think they've driven me mad. Or perhaps it's whatever is inside me causing this." And she held up her hands again.

Grace licked her dry lips. "You're not mad. Just…desperate." The woman was completely insane, but again, it didn't seem prudent to say so. Then she swallowed. "So, you're worried you won't be with us for long. I understand. What do you need my help with?"

Abernath scooted forward, her eyes wide and wild. "Announce that Daring owns a share of the Den of Sin club. Force him to be public about his dual life. Then he can know some of my pain."

Grace took a deep breath. She'd heard of Abernath's affliction before, though she didn't know the name. The welts were thought to be caused by a weak constitution, especially when they were accompanied with madness. Was that the reason the woman was so unstable or was it her past? "I understand. He hurt you and now you want to make him pay." Her heart hammered in her chest. Was there any point in reasoning with a suffering woman? "But I'd like to ask you a question. Besides your personal satisfaction, do you have another goal in mind with your plan? Is there something you hope to accomplish?"

Abernath gave her a sidelong glance. "I..." She pressed her hands together and then winced, setting them in her lap. "I need money."

Grace started to frown but then caught herself. Money? That wasn't madness, that was greed. While less dangerous it was somehow less satisfying as well. "So, you want me to help you blackmail the Duke for money?"

Abernath's face twisted. "I want you to help me provide a future for my son."

Grace's stomach dropped. When Abernath had kidnapped her sister, the house had caught fire. Abernath had fled, leaving an ill-kept child in the house. Her sister and her new husband had adopted the child knowing he could never return to Abernath. Now the crazy woman wanted to provide for him? Grace couldn't believe it was true.

BENJAMIN STYLES, as he'd been called the first twenty years of his life, rode the horse he'd absconded from a passerby as fast as the tired animal would go, which was not all that fast. The Baron of Baderness —it still amazed him that he'd acquired that title—hadn't seen the carriage he'd been chasing in almost an hour.

His stomach clenched in fear. He couldn't lose Grace now. How could he ever go home and face her family or his friends if he lost the woman he'd been assigned to protect? How could he face himself?

Leaning out over the animal's neck, he urged the beast to go faster. He prided himself in being a man of honor. Even in a world often mad with greed and lust, he tried to hold his head above all the riffraff and conduct himself in a manner befitting his title.

Sure, he ran a gaming hell that fed men's worst afflictions. First, he believed that was their vice, not his. And second, he amended that as a former street urchin, he was particularly suited to keep the peace in such an establishment. In fact, he liked to think he kept all those men safer for his efforts. If not for his club, they'd likely participate in the same behaviors at another place. And that place would not have a man who'd acquired his particular set of skills.

Fear pulled at his chest. Though, one other man did possess his skill set, almost exactly. Crusher was the only name by which he'd ever known the man. They'd been fighters together and now they owned rival clubs.

He'd never liked the man—a big, mean, dumb fellow with a giant chip on his shoulder about his success. And now he'd taken the most beautiful woman in all of London.

Bad could confess, at least to himself, that the sight of Grace made every muscle in his body tense and his breath stall in his throat. Why did he have to be so attracted to her? It complicated everything.

But his thoughts focused once again on her rescue. He'd worry about his bloody feelings later. The carriage came into view, rumbling ahead of him as it bounced along the road. The sun glistened off polished wood, the distinctive pattern of carved horses flashing in the light.

Who used a carriage like that to stage a kidnapping? Not that Bad was complaining. It made tracking them exceptionally easy. Even the one time the carriage had nearly lost him, multiple passersby had been able to point him in the direction of the vehicle.

In Bad's opinion, the choice of carriage highlighted both Crusher's arrogance and stupidity. He'd enjoy making that man suffer when he got Grace back.

Crusher turned back from his seat and caught sight of Bad. Bad watched, his muscles clenching, as Crusher reached across the seat and then lifted a pistol from next to him on the seat and leaned back to fire.

The blast filled the air. Bad ducked low over the horse as a ball of lead whizzed by him. He had two choices: fall back again and wait until they surely stopped or surge ahead.

Just then, Abernath leaned out a carriage window, also holding a pistol in her hand.

She leveled the gun toward him. Bad pulled the pistol from his own waistcoat and fired at the same moment she did. Burning pain whizzed through his leg. He looked down to see blood oozing down his pants. Still, he also noted the wound was on the fleshy exterior of his thigh.

Abernath, however, let out a scream and ducked back in the carriage. Not a moment later another scream cut the air. Cold dread washed through him. Grace.

CHAPTER TWO

GRACE SAT in horror as Abernath slid back into the carriage, massive amounts of blood pouring from her shoulder. She thought a scream might have wrenched from her lips but she couldn't be certain.

When the first shot had split the air, Abernath yanked a gun from her skirt. The soft woman pleading for help was gone. In her place, Abernath had given Grace a cold, hard stare as she pointed a pistol at her chest, ordering her not to move a muscle.

Grace had done as she'd been bidden. If she had a goal in this crazy mess, it was to make it out alive.

Abernath slumped over in the seat, the gun dropping to her side. Grace licked her lips, then turned toward the window, peeking out behind her. Her heart jumped in her throat. Bad rode toward them. Without thought, she wrenched open the door. Evening was falling, could she just jump out of the carriage, unseen?

But they were moving with amazing speed and fear seized her again. Bad spurred his horse faster and another shot rang out overhead causing her to crouch down from the opening while still able to view the road behind her. Bad veered wildly and then pulled another pistol from his belt. Grace watched as he took aim and fired.

For a moment, nothing happened. Grace held her breath wondering what came next.

A large thud shook the carriage and she nearly screamed again as the body of Crusher tumbled onto the dirt road, the carriage screeching and veering wildly.

Bad swerved around the man then whipped his horse again, moving closer as the carriage continued down the road. Grace crouched in the doorway, uncertain of what to do.

"Help me," Abernath moaned behind her. "Please."

Frowning, Grace looked back at the woman. For a moment, she wanted to tell the countess she didn't deserve help. After all, the woman had just pulled a gun on Grace. But then she focused on the other woman. Blood pooled on the seat and dripped to the floor and all thoughts of anger fled. Abernath wouldn't survive the wound. She turned back into the carriage but stopped again as Bad came abreast of the door. "Don't move," he yelled. "I've got to stop this carriage."

Tears of joy at the sight of him filled her eyes. He'd come for her. "Thank goodness you're here," she said gripping the door.

He nodded brusquely as he spurred the animal faster, shooting alongside the other horses.

Grace turned into the carriage and began ripping strips from her petticoat. Taking a deep breath, she crossed the tiny interior. "Let me bandage you."

Abernath held up a hand. "Don't touch me."

"I won't hurt you," Grace answered. "You asked for help."

Abernath stared up into Grace's eyes still holding her arm out between them. "I wish I could be you, do you know that? Beautiful, fresh, clean." Abernath's eyes drifted closed. "I should have married Darlington. I did love him. Will you tell him that for me? I didn't mean to hurt him. I just could never trust that he'd love me in return. I was always trying to keep multiple options open in case he changed his mind." The woman closed her eyes. "So many mistakes."

Grace winced. "Cristina, that's your name isn't it?" Cristina had caused the Duke of Darlington a great deal of pain with her cheating ways. "He forgave you those sins a long time ago. It's the new ones that are troubling him." Like kidnapping several Chase women, she wanted to add, but kept that thought to herself.

Cristina grimaced, slumping further down on the seat. "I never could trust a man to take care of me. Not after my father…"

Grace made no response. The carriage was slowing and she partially stood to wrap up the wounds.

"I told you, don't touch me," Cristina closed her eyes. "I don't want you to catch whatever it is I have."

That made Grace stop. "I can't let you bleed out."

"I want to bleed out," Cristina whispered. "It will be a quicker, far less painful death. I just need you to help me first."

"All right, I'll help you," Grace answered, sitting back down on the seat. "What do you need?"

"I want you to expose the club, remember?" Cristina's eyes popped back open and she stared at Grace.

"I'm not doing that. What else?"

Abernath grimaced. "If he's part of the club, Darlington won't see how he should be living his life. He won't see that he needs a family and…"

"Cristina," Grace whispered. "He already sees that. He's talking about selling the club. And he and Minnie are going to start a family."

"And Harry? Will Darlington raise him? Is that where my boy is now?"

Grace shook her head. She did love her son after all. "Not Darlington. But Malicorn. He had a very strained relationship with his father. He wants Harry to have the sort of childhood he never had. He and my cousin, Cordelia, wish to raise the boy. They've already taken him on a tour to meet the extended family. He's likely being spoiled right now."

Tears welled up in Abernath's eyes and Grace watched as one rolled down her cheek. "Cordelia? The one I took to my house? Oh, she's lovely. Kind. I bet she'll make an excellent mother."

"The club's proceeds are going to Harry's estate. They know Abernath was in debt. It will give Harry the title from your husband and the wealth he needs to sustain it."

"What?" Abernath tried to sit up. "But five lords own the club."

"Yes," Grace answered. "And I believe they're all in agreement. They'll provide Harry with an inheritance."

Cristina shuddered and, for a second, Grace thought she was dying. But then another tear slipped down her cheek. "I should have married Darlington," she said again. "He's the one decent man I ever knew."

"Grace," Bad rumbled from the doorway. Grace jumped, only just realizing the carriage had completely stopped. "Come here, love."

She looked to the doorway, her gaze meeting the dark pools of his. Not even pausing, she flung herself from the seat and at his chest, wrapping her arms about his neck.

Had she said he wasn't that handsome? In this moment, he was the most magnificent male she'd ever encountered in her life. Tall, dark, broad shoulders that might very well be able to hold up the whole world, at least hers. And he'd rescued her. "Bad," she cried as her body pressed to his and he pulled her from the carriage, wrapping his arms about her waist. "You came."

But he didn't have a chance to answer. Another shot rang out and she felt the heat and rush of air as the lead ball whizzed by her left ear. Without a second's hesitation, she was thrust back into the vehicle even as Bad pulled another pistol from his waist.

BAD GRIMACED. Not because someone had shot at him. It was the third time that day, he'd been fired upon. And frankly, he'd lost count of how many times someone had leveled a pistol at his chest.

He scowled because he'd had to shove Grace back in the carriage and no one had ever felt so good curled against his chest.

Letting out a long breath, he peeked around the door to determine the shooter's location. While Bad couldn't believe Crusher hadn't died from either the shot or the fall, he knew the man had been the one to try and hit him again. "Where are you, Crusher? Why not come out and fight me like a man?"

He heard Grace's gasp from the interior, but he continued to scan the road behind them. Several rocks and trees lined the dirt road giving Crusher ample hiding spots.

"Come out? Do you think I'm daft?" the other man called. "Might not be as smart as you but I'm smart enough to know how to beat you."

Bad rumbled a dissent deep in his chest. "Really? I'd thought you'd want one last opportunity to beat me man to man and fist to fist." He was baiting Crusher and he knew it. The man had one thing that was larger than his hulking frame and that was the need to prove how good he was.

But this time, he didn't take the hook. "You weren't shot and you didn't fall from the carriage. Even I know I'm in worse shape than you."

"Well, if we're counting wounds, I was shot, actually."

"What?" This was not from Crusher but from Grace. She stuck her blonde head back out of the carriage, scanning him up and down until she spotted the oozing wound on his leg. Covering her mouth, she started to move toward him again.

But he held her back with a single raised palm. "Stay there."

A tear slid down her cheek, resting on her kid glove. "But you're hurt."

He wanted to close his eyes and hold her, but he resisted the urge for several reasons. The most important was that she was safer in the vehicle. But he'd never held her until just a minute ago, and it had become painfully obvious that touching her was a mistake.

Grace might be a spoiled debutante, but he was a street urchin at heart and he didn't deserve to lick the mud from her boots. He'd always known that. Only, she'd felt as good as she looked. Soft and so perfect, smelling of fresh wind with a hint of the sea.

"You don't want me to move," Crusher replied as though Bad had been talking to him. But he clearly had drawn closer, Bad could tell by the sound of his voice.

He raised his pistol. "Grace," he hissed. "Get down."

She obeyed without comment and he said a prayer of thanks for small favors. In all the time he'd guarded her, he wasn't certain she'd ever done what he'd asked of her.

"You're not going to save her," Crusher answered. He was on Bad's left. He could hear that now.

"Why's that?" Bad asked, wanting the other man to keep talking.

"It's my turn to win. And when I do, I'm going to keep your woman for myself. She's a pretty one, she is, and I think I'd like to touch something that pretty. But don't worry, I'll think of you when I do."

Blood rushed in his ears as an anger Bad had never experienced before roared in his veins. Dimly, he was aware that this sort of emotion was dangerous. It would cause him to make mistakes. But Grace was far too fine a woman for Bad himself to touch, let alone for Crusher to put his meaty hands on.

At that exact moment, Crusher stepped out from behind a tree. Bad pointed his pistol but before he could fire a shot rang out behind him, the acrid smell of sulfur filling the air.

Crusher dropped to the ground and a moment later, a dull thud sounded from the carriage. "Oh Cristina," Grace cried.

Bad looked back. What the bloody hell had just happened?

CHAPTER THREE

GRACE STARED at the woman who'd crumpled into a ball on the floor. She covered her mouth to keep from crying out. Cristina Abernath was dead. She'd used her final breaths to shoot Crusher.

"Grace?" Bad growled. "Are you all right?"

"I'm fine," she squeaked. "Can I please come out?"

By way of answer, he leaned into the carriage, reaching for her. She didn't hesitate but launched herself against him, burying her face into the crook of his neck. He smelled of sandalwood, leather and horse, his strong arms wrapping tightly about her. Briefly, it occurred to her that she never wanted to be anywhere else but right here pressed against his chest.

Words she hadn't even planned began tumbling from her lips. "I'm so sorry I was such a fool. I'm sorry I wanted to go shopping. Sorry I let silly ribbons endanger us all."

He chuckled, the sound moving his chest up and down, her own body moving with his and the sound vibrated through her. "I don't know that I ever expected to hear you say sorry."

She tipped back then, to look in his eyes. "Most men might say something like, *Grace you couldn't have predicted this.* Or, *It's all right. I'm here for you.* But not you."

"There's the Grace I know," he said with a small smile.

She gave her foot a small stomp but didn't move away from Bad. Angry as he made her, the world was far too frightening to be anywhere other than wrapped in his arms. "You're making it sound as though I am to blame."

He reached up and brushed a stray hair from her cheek. The touch was achingly gentle. "You're not at fault." His thumb stroked down her cheek to the corner of her mouth. "I'm sorry too. Sorry I lost my temper in the carriage and sorry that I stormed out."

"Oh." She caught her breath. "I didn't expect to hear you say sorry either."

He gave her a small smile that lit his entire face and crinkled his eyes. "Look at us. Apologizing."

"What happens next?" she asked, not wanting to look anywhere other than his face. Up close like this, she could see that his skin wasn't rough, per se, but covered in a number of small scars.

"We find the next town and send men back for the carriage and the bodies."

Grace shivered. In his arms, she'd momentarily forgotten the reality of the day. "Cristina," she whispered. "That poor woman."

"You know that she just stole you from your family?"

Grace lay her head on his chest. "She also shot Crusher before he could shoot you."

"That's what happened?" He gathered her closer, setting his cheek on top of her head. "I'd wondered."

Sighing, she buried her nose in the strong muscles of his chest. "To be fair, I don't think she appreciated his comments about me, but still…I'm glad she did it so that you weren't shot again."

He kissed the top of her head. "Me too."

"Are you very hurt?" she asked, her words catching in her throat. Bad made her crazy with irritation but she found the idea of him dying gut-wrenching.

"No, barely a flesh wound," he murmured into her hair. "Now, let's get you to the nearest town. You need food and rest."

She nodded against his chest, not sure she wanted to go anywhere.

That meant moving out of his arms. Later she'd remember all the reasons he irritated her. Right now, she liked it here. "How will we get there?"

"We'll take Crusher's carriage."

"And Cristina?" Grace gulped. Somehow, she felt some sympathy for the woman and hated to leave her. "I don't think I want to leave her body on the side of the road. I know she's been awful but I…I feel sympathy for her too."

"We'll take her with us if you'd like." Bad's fingers stroked down Grace's neck. "You'll ride on the bench with me."

"Thank goodness," she answered taking a deep breath, drawing in his scent. "I didn't want to leave her but…"

"I understand."

She slipped her hands around his waist, which was amazingly slender compared with his shoulders. "Hello there," a voice called from behind them. Before she could even process, Bad pushed her behind him.

"Who goes there?" he called out, pressing her to his back.

"No need to worry, neighbor. Theodore Bigsby is my name and when I'm not the butcher in the village just north of here, I'm a constable. Do you need assistance?"

"This man, he tried to take my wife," Bad answered pointing toward Crusher.

A jolt of excitement, or perhaps surprise, shot through her at the word wife. Grace craned her neck to see over Bad's shoulder. The butcher was a giant fellow, big and strong, and she shrank closer to Bad's back, placing her hands at his waist.

"That's your wife behind you?" Mr. Bigsby asked. Grace nodded against Bad's back. He was right, it was far simpler to explain if everyone thought them married. But then she realized he couldn't hear her. So, peeking over his shoulder she answered. "Y-Yes sir."

Then she stepped up to Bad's side. Without a word, his arm came about her shoulders. She marveled at how natural this action felt. "He…" she pointed down at the ground, "he shot my friend."

Bad jolted against her but didn't say a word as the constable began to assess the scene. "Your friend, she was defending you?"

"That's correct," Grace answered looking up at Bad. His nose was a bit crooked, almost as though it had been broken. She'd thought it unattractive at first but as she looked now, it occurred to her it was quite masculine.

The constable nodded. "Do you mind transporting them both into town in the carriage? We'll get this whole business sorted quickly and have you both settled into the inn by nightfall."

Grace swallowed. An inn? With Bad? Why hadn't that occurred to her before now?

———

BAD GLANCED over at Grace as she sat on the bench next to him. Bloody hell, the woman was beautiful. Steal-the-breath-from-a-man's-lungs sort of pretty. Her attractiveness never ceased to amaze him.

Even more amazing was the way she clung to his arm. As though he were the only solid structure in a windstorm. She had both her slender arms wrapped about one of his.

Drawing in a steadying breath, he made a note to himself. This was temporary. She didn't like him and she'd return to her senses as soon as she was back with her family.

Besides, gorgeous as she was, he found her annoying. Or perhaps what he found bothersome was the fact that a woman like her would never really care about a street urchin like him. He'd learned to mask his low upbringing and he avoided many social engagements with his now peers. He'd learned in the early days of his barony that the upper class carefully watched every move and looked for any excuse to scorn. Sooner or later Grace would see through his thin veneer.

"We're nearly there," he said into the stretching silence.

"How can you tell?" she asked, lifting her head from his shoulder.

He reached over and placed an arm about her shoulders. She must be exhausted. "The houses, they're growing closer and closer together." Then, as if in answer, the main street of the village came into view.

In short order, the constable took over the carriage and Bad brought his horse to the stable. Then he walked Grace up the steps of the inn and quickly secured them a room and a private dining room.

The innkeeper's wife brought them bowls of stew and freshly baked bread. Grace picked at her food.

Bad frowned, watching her. "You should eat, love. You must be starving."

She looked up, her eyes shadowed and hollow. "I'm tired. And after what happened today…"

He reached across the table, though doing so meant asking for trouble. Every time he touched her, he wanted her a little more. She was like all the shiny things he's seen as a child that he'd known could never belong to him. Except for once, when he'd stolen a penny whistle. He'd loved the toy with all his heart but had been compelled to hide it whenever any adult passed, afraid they'd realize a child in rags could have never purchased such a toy on his own. The hiding had eventually ruined his enjoyment and he'd vowed never to steal again.

"A little bit of food will help you sleep and speed your recovery. Eat for me, love," he said.

She nodded and dutifully dipped the spoon in the bowl, placing a delicate bite into her mouth.

Even the way she ate looked so civilized. Not like him. He stared at the spoon clutched in his hand and slowly, he slipped his hand from hers. Bad shouldn't touch her like this. But her fingers gripped his tighter. "Did you book one room or two?"

"They only had the one. My apologies." He wanted to bring her fingers to his lips. He wanted to put distance between them. He gave his head a small shake.

But she leaned toward him. "I'm glad. I don't want to be alone."

He didn't answer as she finally slipped her fingers from his and tore off a piece of bread to dip into her stew.

He cleared his throat and leaned in. "It's been a very trying day."

Grace leaned toward him too, some color already returning to her face thanks to the stew. "I want to thank you for coming after me. I don't know what I would have done if you hadn't."

He swallowed, not necessarily wanting to say this but sure he'd do better to push her away now, before she stole even more of his affection. "Vice and Ada followed too. I just got here quicker." Vice had fallen behind because her cousin, Ada, had insisted on helping in the rescue. Not only had they been in a slower carriage, but Vice likely stopped further back on the road to allow Ada to rest. He had his own Chase woman to care for. And Bad suspected, when they found each other again, Vice would be engaged to be married. Abernath really had wreaked havoc on them all.

She shook her head, taking another bite. "If I take two more bites may we go up to our room?"

"Yes," he answered, nearly smiling. She made it sound as though he were her father or perhaps her husband. His gut clenched and his smile vanished. He was going to have to share a room with her tonight. How in the world would he manage to be near her and keep his hands to himself?

A knock sounded at the door. Bad turned as the innkeeper stepped into the room. "The constable is here to see you."

Bad nodded as the constable stepped into the room. "Just wanted to let you know that I've taken care of everything for the night but if you could meet me at the church in the morning, we can discuss the arrangements for your wife's friend."

Bad stared at the other man. Why hadn't he realized that he was going to be responsible for transporting Abernath's body back to London? "Of course."

Grace gave a tiny squeak from the across the table, which he ignored until the room emptied again. Then he turned to her, irritation replacing the attraction he'd been fighting. Which was the way it often was with Grace. "Why did you tell them that Abernath was your friend?" Grudgingly, he realized it was easier to push her away like this.

Her spoon dropped into her stew. "You're welcome," she hissed back.

This was how they usually were. "I beg your pardon?"

She picked up her spoon and took a large bite, taking her time as she chewed. Then after making him wait a ridiculously long time, she finally answered. "It was far easier to explain without adding a female villain," she finally answered, scooping out another bite, but she paused before she brought it to her mouth. "And, Harry never need know what his mother has done. I know he'll be happier for it."

He sat back in his chair, as he stared at her. Well those were both bloody good points and he'd successfully managed to push her away again. He ought to congratulate himself, but sick dread filled his insides instead.

CHAPTER FOUR

GRACE STEPPED into the small room and assessed the tiny bed. She'd been glad he was going to be so close. Today, the Baron of Baderness was a boon, a lifeline in a world gone topsy-turvy.

But the man she was about to share this miniscule space with was…large. She consoled herself that at least he'd be close.

"I'll leave you to undress?" he asked as he closed the door behind them. He nearly bumped into her back as she stood next to the bed.

"No," she quickly answered, turning around and looking up into his face. The tight space made her feel off balance and she reached for his shoulder. When had she gotten so comfortable touching him? "I'll sleep in my clothes."

He quirked a brow. "You're dressed for shopping. That can't be comfortable."

She shook her head, looking down at her pale blue muslin gown. It now had streaks of dirt running down the lovely fabric. "I don't see any other way."

He lifted his hands and, for a moment, she thought he was going to pull her into another embrace but then he began working on the delicate buttons running down her back. She gasped and tried to step back but bumped into the bed. He held her still to keep her from falling. "Grace. I just thought we'd remove your outer dress and corset so you might sleep more comfortably."

"Oh…yes. Of course." But her skin heated at the idea of him, of all people, removing her clothes. His hands were big. Not beefy or thick, in fact he had long tapered fingers. But they were just as large as the rest of him. Grace couldn't imagine how they so easily undid tiny little buttons but in mere seconds, her dress was gaping off her front. And though no more of her skin was exposed, she felt open and raw, undressing like this in front of him.

But he paid her embarrassment no mind as he tugged the sleeves from her arms and then, shimmied the fabric over her hips. When he stood up, he reached for her corset strings.

Her heart, which was racing in her chest, stopped at the thought of him removing such a delicate garment. "I can do it myself." She held a hand to his chest to stop his movements but her fingers came into contact with rippling muscle. Somehow that might have been even worse.

"Very well." He took a step back to give her room and pressed his back to the door. Somehow that was even worse. He was near enough to touch her and could watch her every movement as though she were undressing for him.

She huffed a little breath, attempting to cover her reaction. Yes, she was out of sorts, but Grace was also warming in several places. "Close your eyes."

He quirked a brow and then dutifully covered his face with his hands.

Quickly, she undid the strings and dropped the garment on top of the dress. She did her best to pick up the clothes and drape them on the end of the bed before she dove under the blankets. "You can open your eyes again."

She snapped hers closed so that she didn't have to see whatever he was about to do. But her ears were perked to attention and she listened as he shrugged off his coat.

One eye peeked open and she watched as the muscles in his shoulders rippled as he worked the knot in his cravat. Finally coming undone, he added the garment to her pile of clothes and then undid the top of his shirt.

He crossed over to stand by the window. "Go ahead and sleep Grace, I'll get some rest later."

"Later?" she asked, partially sitting up. "When? Where?" She looked about the room. There was very little space to sleep.

He gave her a glance over his shoulder. "On the floor."

"The floor?" She sat up gripping the covers to her chest. That was the most ridiculous thing she'd ever heard. "We'll switch in the middle of the night so that you can have the bed. You can't sleep on the floor."

He turned back to her. "I've slept in far worse places." Then he hesitated. "But thank you for your concern. It's a most unexpected treat."

She dropped the blankets and narrowed her gaze. Never had a thank you sounded more like an insult and her skin bristled with irritation. "Unexpected? Basic human kindness is unexpected from me?"

"Grace, I didn't mean it like that." He held up his hands. "You're not exactly known for thinking—"

"I'm not known for thinking?" Her voice hitched higher with every word. Did he know how insulting that was? "One of us isn't thinking right now, only that person is not me." She'd scrambled to her knees on the bed, her hands on her hips.

"You're not going to storm out of the room and get kidnapped again, are you?" he scoffed, clearly pointing out a time she hadn't really thought her actions through. "Or demand that all of us go shopping when known criminals have been chasing us? You know that I've been shot. Jack was shot. Because you needed ribbon."

Shame and irritation burned down her throat. "I'm to blame for Countess Abernath and her lackeys targeting us?"

"Well," he paused. "No, I suppose not. But a shopping trip under the circumstances was ridiculous."

His chin rose in triumph and hers dropped in defeat. He had her there. She'd been trapped in the house for weeks and she'd just wanted a little trip out. And she'd wanted to be beautiful. Because a lord with a crooked nose was escorting her to balls and.... She nearly gasped. She'd wanted to impress him. She was supposed to be finding a suitable husband. Not a rakehell. "Sit down and take off your pants."

"I beg your pardon?" Even in the dim light of the single candle, Grace would swear that his face paled.

"You heard me. Pants down. Sit." And she pointed at the bed.

HE WASN'T sure where this conversation had gone wrong, but from the moment it had started, he'd felt as though he was on a runaway carriage with no reins. In fact, he was fairly certain he'd rather face Crusher again then Grace.

First, because he'd never had the right words when it came to highborn ladies. They wanted flowery declarations and he'd always been more of a doer, a fighter rather than a poet. Second, because he just couldn't keep up with her. She knelt on the bed, the candle behind her making her chemise see-through so that he could see the curve of her hips, the spread of her legs, the ample shape of her bosom. He swallowed again. And after arguing, now she wanted him to take his pants off. It very nearly resembled a recurring fantasy he had, only he was relatively sure that the woman in his dreams wasn't nearly as beautiful as the one before him. "Grace, I don't think removing our clothing is a wise choice."

She huffed a breath that told him he'd said the wrong thing again. "I need to check your wound. I've been remiss by not looking at it sooner." Then she pointed down to the bed. "Sit."

The wound was fine and furthermore, removing his pants was an awful idea, but he couldn't disobey her. As though he were powerless to deny her demands he reached for the falls of his breeches and pulled down the garment a few inches to take the single step to the bed. He pulled the pants down to just below the wound and sat on the bed, trying to keep the color of his face from turning a bright shade of red. He wasn't certain but he thought he failed.

He'd lost count of how many women had seen him with his pants down but none of them were Lady Grace Chase. "I've had deeper scratches."

She frowned as she looked at his skin, then she reached out and touched his outer thigh, her gentle fingers testing the flesh.

His eyes squeezed closed. Lord help him, but he wanted to tumble that woman into his arms and kiss her senseless.

"We should get some whisky and at least treat the cut," she said as she continued to examine his skin. Then she let go. "And I'll tell you again that I'm sorry I dragged everyone shopping."

He heard the tremble in her voice. "Love," he whispered. "I'm sorry I said that. You're right. It wasn't your fault." It took every muscle in his body to keep from reaching for her and pulling her close. She shouldn't have forced the issue but she wasn't responsible for what happened either.

She sat back, her hands clasping in front of her and her head bent. Her tongue darted out to lick her lips, which made his already-aching muscles taut as a string on a bow. "I just thought that if I could marry like the rest of my sisters, I'd be safe and you'd be free of me. I know you don't like spending time with me but clearly my efforts had the opposite of the intended effect."

He couldn't hold back anymore and he reached out cupping her cheek in his hand. She was so close and wearing so little and he...well, his pants were down around his knees. "Do not rush into choosing a husband and Abernath is no longer a threat. Once I get you home, you won't need to see me ever again." Why did that idea make his chest ache? But he already knew. He liked touching her, looking at her, and increasingly, he liked being with her. Unfortunately, she didn't feel the same.

She let out a loud sigh. "Not see you again? Don't be ridiculous. Your friends are married to my sisters and cousins. Except for Vice and Ada of course."

Vice and Ada? He'd left them on the road alone together. Damn it all to hell. It was on the tip of his tongue to tell Grace what he'd done but she might well demand they go searching for them. Despite his assertion his leg was fine, it throbbed and he was bone-tired after chasing her all day. They'd leave in the morning and try to find the rest of their party. "I'll go get the whisky." He hauled himself off the bed and refastened his pants. "Lock the door behind me."

She nodded as he headed out the door. He heard the lock click behind him. After making his way downstairs, he penned a quick note to Vice. He should say more but he didn't like leaving Grace alone. Folding the paper, Bad instructed the innkeeper to try every inn between here and London until he found a blond man travelling with a redhead who'd answer to the name Vice. He'd pay double the rate if it were delivered tonight.

The innkeeper assured him the job would be done and Bad left, heading for the bar, where he purchased a bottle of whisky. Making his way back up the stairs, he found his chest tightening in anticipation. Bloody Christ, why was he so excited to see her? He'd only been apart from her for mere minutes.

"Grace," he called as he knocked on the door. "It's me."

He heard the lock unclick as she opened the door. She'd undone her hair while he'd been gone and it hung down over one shoulder in silky blonde waves that left him stunned. He only realized he was staring when she blushed. "I was about to braid it. I'll finish in just a minute."

He wished he were a poet in that moment. Wished he could tell her how lovely a shade the color was or how beautiful the texture. But all he could muster was a grunt of, "That's all right."

She stepped back and he entered the room, closing the door and locking it behind him.

"Sit on the sill," she instructed. "May I use your cravat to catch any liquid that flows down your leg?"

"Of course," he answered and attempted to scoot by her while not touching her. He failed. His arm brushed the spun gold of her silky locks and, quite without meaning to, he lifted his fingers to brush the strands. Then, like a school boy, he nearly sighed with delight at their feel.

If she noticed, she didn't let on, and he continued moving until he was on the sill with his pants down once again.

Even more alarming, with his clothing in her hand, she crouched down in front of him. His cock twitched and he gritted his teeth. She was most decidedly a virgin and not ready for his rutting lust. He closed his eyes and willed his body back under control. Fortunately, cold burning liquid scorched down his leg, making him forget his feeling of need. When he opened his eyes again, she'd stood, still holding the bottle. "There," she said. "You're done."

He drew in a deep breath. If she didn't go to sleep soon, he might not survive the night. "Now, why don't you take a drink? Just a small one. It'll help you fall asleep."

She shook her head, staring at the liquid. "I couldn't."

"Trust me," he replied, standing. He reached for the bottle and wrapped his fingers about hers. "Just one small sip will help you sleep. No more than that."

She squinted her gaze. "I've heard that spirits lower your inhibitions."

"They can," he said.

"Is that why you want me to drink?" She squared her shoulders, looking up at him with large blue eyes. "Are you attempting to take advantage of me?"

CHAPTER FIVE

IRRITATION MADE her fingers tighten on the bottle. Why on earth had she just said that? They'd been alone in a room together for over an hour. He'd not done a single inappropriate gesture. The only one of them who was struggling seemed to be her.

While pouring whisky on his bare skin, she'd longed to run her hands over the dark hair dusting his legs. Truth be told, she'd wanted to taste the whisky wetting his flesh. Her nipples had turned to pebbles and her body ached with need.

Then, he'd gone and touched her, his hand wrapping about hers. If she didn't push him away, she'd likely make a complete fool of herself. She might be an innocent but she knew enough about men to know they preferred to chase a woman and not the other way around.

"You think I'd take advantage of you?" he said between closed teeth.

Her nose wrinkled, and she nibbled on her lip. This was exactly why he didn't like her. She was an idiot. "I…no, of course not, it's just…" What did she say? His breeches were still about his knees, her hair was down, and together they clutched a bottle of whisky. If the *ton* could see her now.

"It's just what?" he asked, leaning closer.

Not sure what to say, the truth was the only thing that came to mind, and that was a ridiculously bad idea, she tipped the bottle to her lips, his hand still wrapped over hers, and took a generous swallow. Which was likely a mistake. It burned down her throat and she instantly began coughing, spraying him all over his chest with the amber liquid.

In response, he used his other hand to pound on her back, as she coughed and spluttered. "It tastes like fire," she finally managed to gasp between choking breaths.

He chuckled as he stopped beating her back to wipe his shirt. "I said a small sip, love. No more."

"I'll never touch the stuff again," she said. She wanted to say more. She'd like to begin by asking him to kiss her. What was it like? Would his kiss feel different from another man's?

"You should get some sleep," he said softly. "Tomorrow will be a long journey back to London."

She nodded as she let go of the bottle, then sat on the bed to braid her hair. Her fingers worked the strands. She looked up to realize that Bad hadn't moved. He stood exactly where she'd left him, still holding the bottle. "Is something wrong?"

"Your hair," he mumbled, bringing the bottle to his lips and taking a long swig. Unlike her, he did not spit the liquid out.

"What about it?" she asked, watching his throat work. Why was that so appealing? She cocked her head as his Adam's apple came back to the spot in the center of his neck. It was just so...masculine. "I know it isn't proper to have it down. So much of this is..."

"It's not that," he said as he took another swig. "It's the most beautiful hair I've ever seen."

"Oh," warmth spread through her from the compliment. Or perhaps that was the whisky. "Thank you." She sat up straighter. She had several questions she wished to ask but she wasn't certain how to begin. "Do men marry women because they like their hair or is the person more important?"

She didn't want to tell him that she was asking because she wanted him but she wasn't certain he felt the same in return. In any regard, she'd marry someone, likely very soon. This was a good opportunity to do a bit of research.

He took another long drink. "Many men have married a beautiful woman they didn't really like simply because she was attractive."

She nodded her head, wanting to ask more. Was he one of those men? Then her own questions began to filter in. Did she want to marry him? Was that why she'd asked? She knew she wanted to touch him. That was for certain.

And he made her feel safe, protected. He was titled, and so attractive she ached from need. And…he kept her on her toes. She found she quite liked that. So many men were a bore. "Thank you for answering." Then she snuggled down into the covers closing her eyes. He was right. The whisky's giddy warmth was settling like a blanket over her limbs.

"Why did you ask?" his weight settled next to hers on the bed as he sat by her feet.

She didn't open her eyes as she let out a yawn. She couldn't tell him all that she'd just thought. He'd likely run from the room screaming. Not only was he a confirmed bachelor but he didn't like her. Though apparently, that wasn't much of a determining factor for men. "Well, despite your assertion that I take my time, when I return to London, I'm going to have to find a husband very quickly after this little adventure or risk having no one at all," she said. "Do you know of any lords who are looking? Could you tell them about my hair?"

SHARP, hot jealousy coursed through him, far stronger than the whisky he'd guzzled down.

He'd like to rage that no other man would ever touch her. He wanted to slide his body along hers and curl her up in the hollow of his, where she'd be safe and secure against the hard ridges of his muscles.

She'd asked if a man would marry a woman he didn't like. He wanted to ask if a woman like her would marry a man who was beneath her if he made her feel safe enough. There was always the possibility that a match between them would be forced. They'd spent the night together. But he didn't mention that either. He was more adept at drinking so he held his tongue.

She let out a deep breath, the sort that told him she was drifting into a deep sleep. He relaxed back along the foot of the bed, taking one more swig of whisky before he set the bottle to the side. Then he leaned back against the wall, her feet pushing into his hip. He closed his eyes. He had no intention of sleeping, he just wanted to rest. Try to recover before the long day tomorrow.

There was little chance that Grace would ride in the carriage, and frankly, he didn't blame her. But that did mean she was going to spend the day pressed to his side once again. He wasn't sure he'd survive it.

A clock bell dinged somewhere in the distance and he counted eleven chimes. He slid to the side so that his head was on the bed, and even though his feet hung off, he couldn't complain. He'd meant it. When you'd slept on a cold stone step, this was quite comfortable.

He didn't mean for it to happen but at some point, he drifted off into a light sleep.

He had no idea how much time had passed but it was pitch black when a whimpering sound woke him from his slumber. The room was dark and Bad struggled to see anything at all.

Another whimper filled the room and then a keening cry. He blinked trying to clear the fog from his brain. "Bad?" Grace called. "Bad. Are you there?"

"I'm here," he answered but she didn't respond, only whimpered again.

"Bad. Please. Please help me."

Bloody hell, she was talking in her sleep and she was having a nightmare. He scooted up the bed, drawing his body along hers. "Grace, wake up. I'm here."

"Bad," she gave another strangled cry. "They're coming for me. Please!"

"Grace," he said more sharply, giving her a shake. "Wake up."

She gasped out a breath and sat partially up. "Bad?" But this time his name was different, rather than a whimper it was a wary question.

"I'm here," he said, holding out his arm to her. "I'm right here. I never left."

"Oh, thank goodness," she cried as she flopped back onto the bed and buried her face in the crook of his neck. "I thought I was alone with them again."

He wrapped her in his arms, his nose and cheek pressed into that glorious mane of hair. "I'm not going to leave you. I promise."

"Please," she whimpered against his skin. "Stay with me."

He breathed in her scent, even more potent from sleep. It occurred to him that he'd never shared a bed to actually slumber with a woman before. Notable since he'd bedded all the rest of them, making Grace different in every way. "Haven't you learned yet that I'm not going to let anything happen to you. Even if that means chasing you halfway across England?"

She gave a hiccupping laugh then. The sort that made her entire body shudder. The covers dulled her curves but he could still feel them. "I'm very lucky," she whispered. "To have a man named Bad as my rescuer."

Her chin tilted up as her head tipped back. He leaned down to tell her thank you but before he could utter the words, her lips fumbled into his. It wasn't the most artful kiss he'd ever experienced but raw passion crashed into him like a wave and he leaned down to take her lips again and then again, each touch only fueling the fire within.

She opened to him like a flower, her lips meeting his, wet and eager, her neck exposed as he trailed his fingers down the slender column. When she moaned, he nearly came undone. "Love," he said, his voice sticking in his throat making it rough and craggy.

She wound her arms about his neck, pushing her breasts further into his chest. Dear lord, help him, this woman was made for a man's attention. Every curve screamed to be touched. "Yes?" she asked. "What do you need from me?"

His eyes rolled back in his head. He needed her underneath him. He needed to tuck her away where no man could touch her ever. But she'd overcome her fear and even he realized she was clinging to him because she'd been so afraid, nothing more. "I need you to go back to sleep."

"What?" she asked, pulling back a bit.

"Grace." Every word hurt. "We'll discuss this in the morning. Right now, you should sleep."

"You're joking," she huffed, pulling her arms from his neck and propping up on one elbow.

He wasn't. But he'd managed to irritate her again. "Your very first time with a man won't be because you've had a bad dream. It will be because you're in love or because you've decided to marry. Trust me. It's better this way."

She stared at him in the dark for several seconds before she finally laid her head back on the pillow. "Sometimes I hate you."

He winced. He believed her.

CHAPTER SIX

G‍race woke to a dim light filtering into the room. A feeling of contentment filled her as she cracked one of her eyes open. Her body was encased in warmth despite the coolness of the air about her. She moved, stretching her toes only to realize that she was pressed against a solid wall.

But it couldn't be a wall because it formed around her body and it was both hard and yet deliciously hot. A flood of memories filtered through her mind. Abernath, the tiny inn, the fact that Bad had rescued her and then rejected her advances last night.

Heat filled her cheeks. His name was Bad, for pity's sake. The very first time she'd met him, now over a month ago, he and his friends had been waiting for women of the evening to arrive. He ran and owned a gaming hell. She wasn't even tempting enough to seduce a man who'd made debauchery his entire life.

She nibbled at her lip. Of course, he didn't want her. Other than being pretty, there was nothing special about her.

"Good morning," Bad's deep voice rumbled behind her and he tightened the arm about her midriff, pulling her closer. Well, that wasn't really possible, he squished her even more to his front.

"Good morning," she replied, giving a sniff at the end.

He stilled. "You're still angry with me."

"I'm not angry," she said staring straight ahead. "This is a completely normal and understandable interaction between a lady and a lord."

He smiled. She felt it against the back of her head where his nose was nuzzled into her hair. "I'm still not used to being called a lord."

"What?" she asked, turning back to him then. What did that mean? But she didn't ask the rest of the question because she'd only just realized she was using his right arm as a pillow. His arm curled around her head brushing a few stray hairs away.

"My father was the younger son to the Baron of Baderness and apparently the black sheep of the family. When he married my mother, they left for London. I don't know how they died but when they did, no one came looking for me."

She gasped, her insides clenching and her hand rested on his chest. "I was four and I knew that my father was the son of the baron. I'm not sure how. But I told the woman who ran the orphanage so and she contacted my family. They still didn't come." He swallowed. "I learned later, she'd demanded money and they thought it some sort of swindle. She was so angry that she tossed me out of the home."

"Bad," she whispered, curling her fingers into his chest. Her own insides twisted and her stomach gave a heave thinking of a little boy tossed out on the streets all alone.

"My given name is Benjamin," he whispered, his eyes meeting hers. "My mother called me Ben."

"Ben." Her other hand came up to cup his cheek. "What happened?"

"I slept in doorways, ran errands for a few pennies for food, survived by cunning and wit, I suppose until I was discovered by Monsieur LaFleur to join his fighting club. I was ten when I began training."

Her throat had nearly closed as she stared up at him, tears stinging in her eyes. All the scars, the crooked nose. He'd been a fighter.

He looked down at her. "I was nineteen when I learned that I was the next male heir to the title." He shook his head. "I may look like a lord now, love. But make no mistake, I'm a street urchin through and through."

Grace stilled. What was he explaining to her precisely? That he wasn't a real lord? Was this an explanation of sorts? But why would he reject her? He had the title and as far as she could tell, he was the most gentlemanly man she knew. "But you're the rightful heir, that was never a question and…"

"I grew up thinking I was trash. Dropped and forgotten, unloved and unwanted even by my own family." His face spasmed, pain in every line.

Grace didn't answer at first. She didn't know what to say. She lifted her head from his arm, looking into his dark eyes. "You grew up strong. I don't blame you if you wish for a different childhood. What you went through is terrible. But it's shaped you into a man who can single-handedly rescue a woman from a runaway carriage while being held captive by multiple villains."

His eyebrows rose, the deep lines in his face easing. "Abernath wasn't a real villain."

Grace shrugged. "You might have me there. She had sores all over her palms and she talked as though she were mad."

Ben drew her head down to the crook of his neck. "That actually frightens me more. I'm so glad you're here and safe."

"I'm glad too," she answered, drawing in his sandalwood scent. There were moments when she felt closer to this man then any other person in England. But then she remembered. This conversation had begun because he'd rejected her last night. She eased out of his grasp. "I'm sure you're eager to return me home."

He searched her face, his hand coming to cup her cheek again. "I've never told anyone that story before. I'm mean, I've mentioned a few pieces but—"

His confession pulled at her heart. "Your secret is safe with me," she answered. "And for what it's worth, I think you're worthier than most to carry the title of lord." She made to roll away and get out the bed but his hands held her firm.

"Do you really mean that?" he asked, his face pitted in deep lines once again as his fingers dug into her back. He held her now like he never wanted her to go. Which she knew wasn't true. They did nothing but argue and he'd rejected her just a few hours ago. He didn't want her and she'd be a fool to think he did.

BAD KNEW that he should let her go. But her words were the balm he hadn't realized he'd needed. Slowly, carefully, she reached up, tracing several of the scars that pitted his face. "Every word," she answered, giving him a small smile. "I'm not sure where I'd be right this very moment without you but I am forever in your debt."

Debt? The word echoed about his brain as he released her and she rose from the bed. He watched her as she sat up, stretched, her back elongating in the prettiest way, her arms tossed over her head.

He knew exactly what he'd do with a man who owed him a debt. He'd collect. And what he wanted from Grace...well, despite his rejection last night, he knew exactly the way he'd like to collect.

His muscles tightened. He wasn't just referring to sex. Though that was most certainly part of it. He thought back to the kisses they'd shared, she'd been so eager and pliant underneath him. But a man did not dally with a woman like Grace without understanding the full measure of consequences.

She began dressing and he lay his head down, unabashedly watching her. Her movements were nimble and filled with a natural grace that made him ache to touch her again. He should look away. It was the polite thing to do, but he didn't want to and he was, after all, still a street urchin at heart, title or no.

Damn, he wanted to touch her. Pull her back into the bed and feel her body underneath his. His fingers dug into the blankets as she reached behind her to tighten her own corset strings. He should offer to help but he'd never complete the job. He'd end up stripping every piece of clothing from her body and kissing her from the tip of her toes all the way to her... He tried to control his errant thoughts.

"How long will it take us to get back?" She turned back to look at him and he tried to make his face a blank mask.

"Seven hours. Maybe eight unless the weather changes." He sat up. He'd never in his life wanted to see rain more. How nice would it be to hold her in his arms another night?

She turned back to him again. "Does my family know I'm safe?"

Her family? He drew in a sharp breath. How had he not thought of her family until now? "I sent a message to Vice. He and Ada are also following us but I'd guess they were travelling at half the speed we were. Once he receives the message, he'll send word to your parents."

Grace gave a stiff nod as she picked up her crumpled dress. "Fitting that this is what I'll wear back into London."

"Why's that?" he asked as he watched her shimmy the gown over her hips. They wiggled back and forth until the gown could pull over them. He raked his fingers through his hair, giving the strands several good tugs. Pain was the only solution to curb his desire.

She faced the window. "My humiliation will be complete." Then she looked back at him. "Unless, of course, you agree to marry me."

Bad's mouth dropped open. "Marry you?" He'd already known this was a possibility. She could be ruined for this little adventure and she had no other options for a husband. But somehow hearing her say the words was different and if he'd taken advantage of her last night… Or rather, if *she'd* taken advantage of *him*. "Is that why you were trying to seduce me last night?"

Her gasp was the first indicator that he'd said something wrong. She flew around the bed, her gown still gaping off her front, then her hand whistled through the air as it landed with a crack on his face. "How dare you?" she shrieked loud enough to wake the dead.

She raised her hand again, but this time he refused to let her hit him. He caught the hand and then she attempted to hit him with the other, which he captured as well. She tried to yank away, twisting wildly and he was honestly afraid she might hurt herself. Giving her a tug, he easily brought her back on the bed where she commenced trying to kick him.

One landed on his shin and with a grunt, he rolled on top of her.

Her head twisted back and forth as her cheeks grew increasingly pink. Rather than deter him, he found the sight rather arousing and when her head finally stopped, he dropped his forehead to hers. "I didn't say I wouldn't."

She stared at him. "You're a beast. You know that."

"I do," he answered.

CHAPTER SEVEN

THE SECOND THE retort left his lips, she knew she'd made a terrible mistake. He'd just explained that he considered himself unworthy.

He deserved her anger. She'd kissed him last night, not because she'd been trying to trap him, but because she couldn't help herself and it hurt to think he considered her a scheming female. How could he lump her with the likes of Abernath? "I didn't mean it like that."

"It doesn't matter," he answered. Suddenly, he jumped off her, rising from the bed.

She gave a loud sniff. "It matters to me." And she rose too. There was little room for him to leave and he started for the door. He wouldn't actually leave her, would he? "Ben," she choked out, fear strangling her voice.

He turned back. "Grace."

"Don't leave me again." She reached for him then. "Please."

He only hesitated a moment before he reached for her, pulling her back into his arms. "I won't."

"I wasn't trying to manipulate you," she whispered. In every interaction, they seemed to hurt one another, and Grace realized she was often attempting to protect herself. But somehow, that wasn't working. They weren't understanding one another. "I just find you to be…"

He leaned back. "What?"

She licked her lips, preparing herself to admit this out loud. "Difficult to resist."

He quirked a brow. "That is encouraging." Then he slowly backed up. "Get dressed. We'll eat and leave within the hour." Then he turned away to ready himself.

Grace frowned at his back. That was it? She'd admitted she was attracted to him and all he could say was that it was encouraging?

She shook her head.

Within the hour, they had, in fact, set off for London. Once again using Crusher's coach, Grace had chosen the ride on the seat next to him rather than inside the carriage. She sat next to him in the cool morning air, with her arms wrapped about her waist. When they'd left after noon the day before, the air had been warm and sunny. And she'd hardly noticed the cold last night. But this morning, it seeped into her bones.

Hunching over, she resisted the urge to snuggle into Ben's side. She knew he'd be radiating heat and comforting physically, of course. But what would she lose for giving him the satisfaction? Most likely, another comment that left her weak with disappointment.

He moved the reins to one hand and shrugged off his coat. He couldn't be hot, could he? She glared at him, as if his very body temperature were set to insult her. Fortunately, she held her tongue as he dropped the coat around her shoulders. "You're freezing."

"Thank you," she murmured, pulling the jacket tight about her. "How's your leg?"

"Fine," he answered, grimacing at the rip in his pants. "But these were my favorite breeches."

She gave a small smile as she reached out a hand from under his large coat to touch the tear. "I can mend them for you. My stitches are quite good. It's one of the few things I am known for in my family."

He looked to her. "What else are you known for?"

"I suppose being pretty."

"You sound as though you don't believe them."

Grace watched the rhythmic beat of the horse's hooves as they plodded down the road. "I don't not believe them. I just don't see what the advantage is. I mean, perhaps there are some. I get asked to dance at balls. Once, when I was a child, my father's friend had gold pearls on his watch chain. When I exclaimed how beautiful they were, he chuckled and gave me one. My sisters were very jealous. When Emily asked why I'd gotten one and she hadn't, my mother exclaimed, "Oh, Emily, try and understand, Grace is just lovely to look at.""

She peaked over at Ben who was frowning. "I can tell by your tone that you find this annoying, but I fail to understand why."

Grace let out a long sigh. "People like me because of my face or my hair. They don't actually like me, not even you."

He grunted. "I never said I didn't like you."

"You didn't have to," she replied.

"Enough of that," he answered. "I like you just fine but you go out of your way to provoke me."

That was most likely true. "You provoke me too."

He looked over to her then. "Do I?"

She huffed a breath. "You know that you do. In fact, you have rejected me twice in the last several hours."

He raised a finger, which in her mind added insult to his words. "I didn't reject you either time, I'm just being prudent."

"Can't you see that a lady doesn't wish for a man to be prudent when discussing their possible future? I'm glad you're weighing your options with me like a transaction. That makes me feel truly special."

"That isn't what I meant," he snapped, slowing the carriage. "You want me now, Grace, after my rescue. How will you feel in a month from now when the fear has faded and you're strapped to a former street urchin?"

"Ben," she gasped. "Is that what you think?"

―――

WHY HAD he gone and revealed how he still couldn't lose the stigma of his past? He'd never shared any of this with anyone and he knew why. In the moment, he'd never been more vulnerable. "I'm not good with words. I wish I was." He gripped the reins tighter. "I learned to read when I became a lord but…" Damn. He was doing it again. Sharing details that he'd never confessed before today.

He squeezed his eyes shut, his chest tight, but then her hand gently wrapped around his biceps. "You're doing marvelously well, in my opinion. I'm practically hanging on your every word."

He swallowed, trying to clear the emotion that clogged his throat. How had she known that's what he needed to hear? "Thank you," he said, leaning down and placing a soft kiss on her cheek.

"You're welcome," she answered. "And just to make this clear, I would be lucky to be strapped to you, so to speak."

He nearly fell from the bench. "You don't mean that—"

Grace gave him a pointed stare. "I do to," she answered, leaning in and placing a kiss on his mouth. Her lips were achingly soft against his.

"Grace, I inherited a failing barony. You could have the richest duke in England. Well, except for Daring. He's already spoken for."

"Is your barony still failing?" she asked, her eyebrows going up as if she were about to make a point.

Damn the woman was hard to argue with. "No. But I used a gaming hell to lift it back up."

She nodded. "Resourceful." And she touched one of her pointing fingers to the other. Then she began counting a list on her hand. "Brave." Middle finger. "Strong." Ring finger. "Honorable." Pinky. "I've got more but I've run out of fingers."

He wanted to stop the carriage, pull her in his lap and kiss her senseless. "In terms of our marriage, it was never a question. I knew the moment I set after you that I may well have to marry you."

Grace cringed and he knew he said something wrong. She likely wanted a declaration of how he wanted to marry her, dreamed of a woman like her. He didn't blame her, but he'd revealed so much, he wasn't sure he was capable of more. Not today.

He braced himself for her anger, but instead, she did something far worse. Her shoulders hunched over. "That hardly seems fair. After risking your life to keep me safe, you're going to be forced into a marriage."

"I didn't say forced," he said, his lips pulling back from his teeth.

Grace didn't reply. Which was somehow so much worse than when she got angry.

They sat in silence for the longest time. An hour, perhaps more. The sky turned grey, which suited his mood perfectly. But just as they reached the next village on the route, it began to rain. Light at first but then fat drops began to shower down over them. Grace did press into his side then and he wrapped an arm about her to keep her dry or at least warm.

By the time they'd reached the stables, it was pouring, soaking their clothes through. "At least my dress will be cleaner," Grace stuttered through chattering teeth.

He smiled even as he reached the public barn, two grooms coming out to greet them. "We'll have to stop until the rain lets up."

She nodded as he helped her down.

It was the only time, in his entire life, that he'd wished for rain. In fact, he'd spent most of his childhood wishing that damn stuff away. But today, he'd be cozy inside a warm room with a soft woman that he might just have to strip down to make sure she'd dried. He had a whole new appreciation for water falling from the sky.

CHAPTER EIGHT

EVEN IN BEN'S COAT, Grace shivered again. Her hair was wet, her cheeks soaked with rain, her dress saturated with water.

Ben helped her from the bench, holding one hand in his much larger palm as his other wrapped about her waist. He didn't even bother to set her down as he sprinted for the inn. A large fire roared in the common room and he set her in front of the flames as he searched out the innkeeper to secure rooms. "We beat the crowds," he said as he returned. "I was able to get two."

Grace frowned. She didn't want to sleep in a bed alone. In fact, she quite liked being tucked against his side warm, safe and so snug against his large frame. "Excellent," she murmured as she spread out her dress, hoping to help the light fabric dry faster.

"I'll get us some stew and then we can go to our rooms." He held out his elbow to lead her to a table.

The stew did warm her but as they headed up the stairs, she immediately began to feel cold again. Her dress was still damp and without the fire, she started to shake again. "I wish I'd known I'd get abducted. I would have worn something more practical."

He smiled as he tucked his arm about her. "You'll have to take off your clothes to dry them out."

"And my hair too," she replied, feeling her wet coif. She'd twisted a braid and pinned it to the back of her head, which had seemed sensible this morning, but now it held in water.

He sucked in his breath, she heard the soft sound and her eyebrows went up. "I'll see if I can't find you a comb."

"Thank you," she answered as he inserted a key into the first door.

"Our rooms connect." He pushed open a door to a room that was much larger than the last they'd stayed in. After dropping her hand from his elbow, he crossed and opened the interior door to the other room. "They are equal size," he reported, standing in the doorway.

Grace shrugged off his coat, hanging it on a peg on the back of the door. There was a fire going and she crossed the room to stoke the flames before she began pulling pins from her hair.

Her back was to Ben but she knew he was still there, standing in the door between their rooms. He hadn't made a sound but she could feel his gaze and her skin heated at the knowledge. The braid unfurled and fell down her back. She pulled off the cloth she'd used to tie it at the bottom and began to pull apart the three sections of hair, shaking them out as she went. When the strands hung down her back like a wet curtain, she looked over her shoulder. "Since you're still here, would you mind helping with my dress?"

He swallowed, his Adam's apple bobbing up and down. Grace felt a pinch of regret. She knew he had an affection for her mane of hair and she was using that knowledge against him.

"Of course," he answered, stepping toward her.

She left her hair swinging down her back, forcing him to push the strands aside. He reached for the hair, letting it run through his fingers before softly placing the silky mass over one shoulder.

Then his fingers began, once again, working the row of tiny pearl buttons. She turned to look back at his face, which in turn pushed some of her hair back in his way. His face tightened as he gently pushed the hair back again.

Her plan was working. She had no intention of sleeping in this room alone and thus far, Ben had been exceedingly good at avoiding her advances. Which had hurt her pride a bit. As did the knowledge that her affection for him was one-sided. Since he'd already proclaimed that he'd marry her, she might as well make sure their union was enjoyable for both of them. The thought of being smitten alone...well that sounded dreadful.

He reached the last button and she shrugged the dress down her arms, pushing it off her body. Ben began untying her corset, which joined the dress on the floor. She grabbed the wooden chair seated at the writing desk and sat, holding up one boot. "Would you?"

Without a word he bent down and began unlacing the boots, pulling the shoes from her feet. When his fingertips grazed down her calf, she smiled even as her insides tightened in anticipation. A breathless excitement fizzled in the air, almost tangible enough to touch.

Grace stood in her stocking feet and reached under her chemise, pulling down the damp pantaloons underneath. She heard him suck in his breath and he reached for her hip, grasping her softer flesh in a tight grip. "Grace," he groaned out, low and guttural. "You go too far."

She looked up at Ben as his dark gaze stared down at her. She pressed her hands to his chest, resting on the hard muscles beneath. "I'm freezing." Her tongue darted out to wet her lips and his gaze followed the movement. "Aren't you going to help warm me up?"

He pulled her closer, his head dropping. "You're a witch, you know that don't you? You're trying to cast a spell on me."

Rather than be insulted, that made her smile. "Is it working?"

"Perhaps," he answered. He searched her face. "What happens when you succeed?"

His question confused her. Wasn't it obvious? They'd marry. She'd stay tucked by his side. Forever. "We'll be together."

He narrowed his gaze even as he shifted away. "What then? I won't tie you to me to have you hate me later." Then he stepped away and, retreating across the room, slammed the door behind him.

BAD KNEW what she was doing. Hell, he even understood why. He'd resisted her thus far but a woman like Grace was used to getting her way. He'd made himself a challenge and she'd accepted.

He needed to be sensible for the both of them. If he allowed her to coerce him into taking her then they'd both be well and truly stuck. Hell, maybe they were already. But right now, there was a chance. Once he bedded her, there was none.

It wasn't that he didn't want her. In fact, he wanted her in the worst way. His whole body ached from need. But he didn't want a wife who hated him. Who looked at him and saw the filthy boy who'd slept in doorways. The man who would never quite fit in with polite society. How would she feel when he used the wrong fork at a dinner party, uttered the wrong words to their host? He'd borne looks of disdain his entire life and he couldn't stand the thought of her disgust. Everyone else's he could bear but not hers.

Pacing the room, he watched the rain and fought with himself. She was his for the taking. Every minute, he considered opening the door again and making her his. How would she taste? He already knew how she felt pressed against him. The memory made him ache.

But then he'd return to his senses. Even if they married, he could be a gentleman now. Somehow, that mattered. As though he could prove to her he was worthy.

After ringing for a servant, he ordered food brought to his room. Taking a deep breath, he knocked on the connecting door. "I've ordered dinner. Are your clothes dry?"

There was a pause. "Mostly," she finally answered.

"Do you need help dressing?" He tightened his fingers on the doorknob. Part of him hoped she said yes while another dreaded the idea of touching her again. He thought back to yesterday. His first intuition had been correct. Every time he grazed her flesh with his fingers, he drew further into Grace's web. There was little chance he'd escape.

The thought made his head fall against the door. It was already too late. He cared for her and no matter what happened, he was likely to get hurt.

"No. I'll be all right," she replied.

Dinner arrived twenty minutes later and he set the tray on the writing desk. The connecting door swung open and Grace walked into his room. He was in trouble. She'd put on her dress but nothing underneath. Her feet were bare; he remembered the slender curve of her calves and ankles. She obviously wasn't wearing a corset, and her natural shape left him near breathless. And her hair. Dear God, it was dry and hanging down her back in shimmering golden waves. She must have undone the strands to help them dry. "Smells delicious." She stopped leaning over the tray and inhaling a big whiff. "Travelling has made me quite hungry."

He was hungry too. But not for the stew. "It smells passable and you should have on your stockings and shoes. These floors must be freezing."

She shook her head. "These fireplaces do a marvelous job of heating the rooms. The floors are quite warm." She gave him a glowing smile. "Shall we eat?"

He narrowed his gaze as he nodded. When she smiled like that, she looked near angelic. He went into her room and retrieved her chair so that they might both sit and when he returned, he found her already ladling out his stew. She was bent over the desk as she worked and his hand ached to run over the curve of her backside.

He closed his eyes as he set the chair down with a decided thud.

"What's wrong?" she asked as she sat in the other chair and he followed suit.

She picked up a spoon, delicately balancing the utensil in her hand. "How do you do that? How do you hold a spoon as though it were a part of your hand?"

She blinked at him, turning her head to the side. Then without a word, she set her spoon down again and stood, padding over the floor in her bare feet. "My mother subjected me to years of decorum lessons followed by finishing school. If either my mother or my instructor, Madame LaVeau, saw me now, they'd drop into a dead faint."

His tongue stuck to the roof of his mouth. "I'm turning you into an urchin too."

She let out a tinkling laugh and then grasped his hand in her own. Sliding his fingers open she curled the middle and pointer finger back together, resting the spoon in his grasp. "Just like that."

He stared at the spoon. It looked ridiculous in his massive hand. "How do you actually eat?"

She pressed her lips together. "It will take practice," she murmured close to his ear. "But I've every confidence you can master it. I've seen you fire a pistol. You've exceptionally dexterous hands."

The hair on the back of his neck stood as her breath whispered across Bad's skin. He'd like to show her another way his hands were quite skilled. But before he could formulate a more appropriate response, she crossed back to her spot and picked up her own utensil. "Shall we?"

He gave a nod. At first, he watched her, then he attempted to use the spoon in the awkward position she'd placed it in his hand. He grimaced. He looked like a fool. Worse yet, there were a thousand instances when he noticed that he did not behave as the other lords did. And she'd see them too just as she'd seen this one.

But she didn't look up as she ate, giving him the freedom to attempt to figure out the awkward positioning without fear of being caught in a mistake. Which surprised him. He hadn't thought Grace could be so subtle, accepting. Verbally, they were always at odds. But now, she wasn't trying to spar with him. Instead, her actions were…supportive.

"Are you the youngest of your sisters?" he asked.

She nodded. "Yes." Then she let out a soft sigh. "Ruined before I even had a season. That takes some doing."

He shook his head. "None of this was your fault."

She looked at him then, one of her eyebrows arching. "Really? That isn't what you said yesterday."

He deserved that. Leaning forward, he returned her stare. "Well, I would appreciate it if you used sense when it came to your own safety."

"Touché," she replied leaning back, her chin tucking into her chest. "Sense, I suppose, is not something I'm known for."

Guilt clogged his throat. Usually, she'd reply back with some sort of smart retort and, to his surprise, he liked their back and forths. "I did not mean to offend."

"I'm not offended." Her head remained down. "You're right. I've always been rash. And sassy."

This Grace, humble, helpful, would undo him. "I love both those qualities about you, except for when they lead to your kidnapping."

She tilted her head up and peered at him for several seconds. "You like them?"

"I like our discussions. Your wit. Your tendency to speak your mind." How had she done this? Now he was listing her finer qualities. "And one person can't be smart, beautiful, funny, and sensible. It simply wouldn't be fair."

That made her smile. A smile that stained her cheeks pink and glowed with gratitude. She stole his breath from his lungs. "Thank you." Then she nibbled her bottom lip. "I have a favor to ask."

He'd been leaning forward as their conversation grew more intimate but he pulled back, needing distance. Somehow, he was fairly certain that he'd just been led like a lamb to the slaughter.

CHAPTER NINE

GRACE NEEDED Ben to say yes. She held her breath as his eyes widened.

"A favor?" he asked.

She could tell, just by the growl in his voice, he'd grown suspicious again. She didn't reply. Yet. With a few hours alone to contemplate, she'd come up with a new plan. First, she'd tried being her sassy self. He hadn't budged. And she'd attempted, when she'd asked him to undo her dress, to be more like Diana. Bold and brave. He'd retreated. So... her next strategy was to be more like her sister, Cordelia. Kind, soft, and understandingly intelligent. It had been working, right until the favor part.

Her stomach clenched, realizing she was failing at acting like her smart sister. Would Cordelia ask a favor? Likely not. "I'm afraid to be alone in my room tonight," she confessed.

He set down his spoon. "Grace, I really should sleep in my own—"

"We could pull your mattress into my room. You'd be comfortable and in your own bed." She reached for his hand and after a moment's pause, he allowed her to clasp his hand in hers. "Please. I'm scared."

He closed his eyes, his muscles tensing. "Love."

She could hear the *no* in the single word. "I won't tell anyone. I swear." And she laced her fingers through his.

He sat looking at their joined hands, indecision making the lines in his face taut. "It's not a good idea."

She rose then, keeping their hands joined, and skirted around the table. She wasn't certain how Cordelia would act now, or Diana for that matter. But she knew what Grace would do.

Grace let his fingers go, then wrapped her arms about his neck and slipped onto his lap. He didn't stop her but he didn't hold her either. Taking his lack of action as consent, she curled into his body, resting her head in the crook of his neck. She was tempted to continue talking. Try to convince him otherwise, but once again, her intuition told her it was best to remain quiet. So, she did.

Slowly, Ben lifted his hands from his sides, one wrapping about her knees, the other resting on her backside.

Tilting her head back, Grace placed a soft kiss on the base of his neck. He shivered under her lips.

"What is it you want from me?" he asked, the rumble of his deep voice reverberating through her.

Grace slid one of her hands up into his hair. The best answer was the truth, though perhaps not all of it. If she confessed her love, he might run screaming in the other direction. "I want you to want me the way I do you."

He squeezed her tighter, lifting her up so that her head tipped back. That was when his lips brushed across hers. Sparks of desire sizzled along her flesh as she clutched his hair. He responded, pressing their mouths together again and again until he slanted her lips apart and brushed his tongue along her bottom lip.

A moan ripped from her lips but he swallowed the sound as he kissed her again, his tongue dancing along hers. Never had anything felt as good as this and she mimicked his gesture, wanting to taste more of him.

He kneaded her bottom's flesh, then caressed his hand up her side until he rested it under her arm where he palmed her breast, weighing the flesh in his hand, finally tweaking the nipple. She arched into the touch, pleasure rolling over her in waves. "Ben," she moaned, her head falling even further back.

Somehow, his name seemed to loosen his control. Suddenly they were up out of the chair, her weight firmly cradled against his chest.

She wasn't aware they were moving until her back came in contact with the mattress but she didn't have much time to think about it, because his weight pressed to her front. Then she knew several things all at once. She belonged under this man. His hips settled between her legs and the hard press of his flesh pushed into her soft womanly parts making her cry out in desire. It curled inside her, making her forget all her fear, worry, and doubts. She wasn't too sassy in this moment, too silly, too vain. He was perfect and he made her feel the same.

Her chemise rode up her thighs, allowing her to wrap her legs around his, creating even more pressure where she needed it most.

He slid his mouth from hers, kissing a trail down her neck as he untied her chemise. His hips were sliding away too and she whimpered out her protest. She wanted his pelvis cradled against hers.

He smiled against her collarbone. "Patience, my love." Then he pulled the chemise to one side, exposing a nipple. When his tongue dragged across the sensitive flesh, her insides convulsed and her fingers dug into his back.

"Yes," she hissed as his mouth closed around the dark skin, sucking it into his mouth.

Then, he reached for her chemise and began dragging the fabric higher up her thigh, his hand stroking her leg as he did so. When the fabric had reached her waist, he stopped, tracing her belly button, before cupping her most private area with his large hand.

Funny, she'd always liked the size of his hands without really understanding why. But now, in this moment, she knew. His fingers touched her everywhere all at once and pleasure near exploded from her insides as she bucked against him.

"Not yet, love. I've got something even better for you."

Better? How could anything be better than this?

BAD HAD DIED and gone to Heaven. That was all he could think as he sucked one of her nipples back into his mouth. Her skin was a shade darker than cream and her nipples were the pink of a pale rose. And her taste…bloody hell she tasted of vanilla. He'd once heard vanilla described as boring, which was ridiculous. It was the perfect mix of earthy and sweet. The sort of flavor a man could happily sip on for the rest of his life.

He slid one of his fingers into her silky wet channel, and it tightened about his digit, causing his cock to pulse with need, his seed leaking from the tip. He was going to spill it at any moment like a damned schoolboy on his first go.

Not that it mattered. He wouldn't take her today and she'd be none the wiser.

Not that he planned to let her go either. Now that he'd taken a bite of her forbidden fruit, he'd not let another man sample it. She was his now. That much was clear.

Kissing a trail across her chest and down her stomach, he wished he'd removed her chemise but he was too impatient to do so now. He wanted to taste the nectar between her legs, and he was growing frantic.

She ruffled his hair, scratching his scalp as she arched her body against his mouth. He'd known touching her would be like this. She was full of spit and vinegar when they argued. He'd known that those tendencies were the sign of a passionate woman. Grace hadn't disappointed.

He kissed over the soft triangle of curls, her hips undulating against him and he wanted to growl in satisfaction. Reaching out his tongue, he took a small sip, just a sampling of her flavor and need rocked through him. She was delicious and so bloody gorgeous that his teeth ached.

"Please," she begged, digging her nails so hard into his scalp, he was certain she'd leave marks. He liked it and he had every intention of teasing her some more.

"You want more?" He gave her another small lick, his muscles tensing from the effort to hold himself back.

She arched again, looking like a goddess. "Yes," she hissed pulling at his dark hair.

Again, another small touch of his tongue. She convulsed under the teasing. "Will you beg?" he asked.

For a moment she stilled, her fingers loosening in his hair and he swore under his breath. If he'd scared her away he'd never forgive himself. It was just that he was growing to like their exchanges, but perhaps it was too soon to bring them into the bed.

But then Grace did something he hadn't expected at all. Suddenly her thighs tightened around his head, her calf hooking his neck and pushing his face closer. "Not beg," she answered, squeezing him tighter. "Demand."

He grinned, damn that little imp and her vivacious personality. He had to confess that he loved it. "Yes, my queen," he rumbled against her thigh and then he licked her fully, flattening his tongue against her sweet flesh.

She moaned and jerked her hips but he didn't decrease the pressure, rather he held her hips in his hands and increased it. Her thighs trembled around his ears as she twisted her head back and forth.

She exploded against him, moaning his name in a loud cry that filled him with satisfaction as his own seed spilled. They hadn't even been together, not fully, and yet this was the single best experience of his life.

Climbing up her body, he lay next to her. "Grace," he whispered, brushing her hair back from her face. He could comb her hair like this for hours.

A sleepy, satisfied grin spread across her lips as she curled into his side. "Yes?"

"You really are a queen." My queen, he thought.

She didn't open her eyes but the smile turned down. "Is it because you think me spoiled?"

He kept brushing her hair back from her face. "Oh, you're that.

There's no doubt. But I was referring to the fact that you could turn me into your willing slave."

Her eyes opened then, one of her pale arms reaching about his neck. "And if I were to demand, as your queen, that you kiss me like that again?"

He trailed his hand down her back. "What my queen wishes for, she gets."

CHAPTER TEN

GRACE WOKE JUST as the sun rose the next morning. She wasn't tucked against Ben but his heat still lingered, making her warm and cozy. Lifting her head, she saw him standing near the window. "Good morning," she mumbled, burrowing deeper under the covers.

"Good morning," he said turning back toward the bed. "I hope I didn't wake you."

"Not at all," she answered, pushing back the curtain of hair that had fallen into her face.

He crossed the room and sat on the bed next to her, combing back the strands with his fingers. "I did find a comb for you. It's on the table."

She nodded. "I saw it last night. I'll put it to good use this morning."

He grimaced, just a hint, before he concealed his expression again. "That's likely a good idea. You'll need to look presentable."

"Presentable? Why? Because I'm returning home today? I was kidnapped, they'll likely understand my disheveled appearance." She rolled onto her stomach, her hands under her head. The idea of going home filled her with a certain dread. She liked being with Ben. More than liked it, she loved being tucked against him and she didn't want all those people, meaning her family, between them.

He continued to comb through her hair, his fingers simultaneously stroking down her back. "Well, you are returning to London today but..." he paused. "This morning I heard a familiar voice in the hall. Woke me from a dead sleep."

She scrunched her brows as she looked up at him. "Heard a voice? Who?"

"Daring," he said. "He's here. And so is Exile and Jack."

She rolled back over, the blankets having been pushed down to her waist. Her chest was exposed to him but somehow, she'd lost any shyness with this man. His eyes devoured her as she lay there. Her tongue darted out to wet her lips. She didn't want her time with Ben to end. "Are you sure you weren't dreaming you heard them? You were asleep."

Ben traced her collarbone then drifted lower over her breast. Her body began to tighten in response. "I'm afraid not, love. Even after I woke, I continued to hear them. They're here and they're looking for us."

She sat up then and he gathered her into his arms. "Why? I'm perfectly safe with you. You'll bring me back and—"

"I didn't have much time to write them a note. It was rather brief. They might be worried that Abernath or Crusher is still chasing us or, perhaps, they just want to protect your reputation by returning together. If no one finds out you've been gone, you might not have to marry me."

Her insides tightened and she pulled away. "But I thought we'd already agreed to marry. I've slept in your bed. I've—"

He held her cheeks in his hands. "I didn't take your maidenhead. You can go to your wedding pure enough."

Her breath caught and filled her chest making it ache. She looked at him, trying to speak but her voice wouldn't work. They'd decided to marry. How could he say this now? Her stomach churned. It was because he didn't want her. She was the spoiled, vain Chase girl and now that he'd had his way with her, he was done. Men thought her pretty, but no one actually wanted her for marriage. Why would he be any different? "You would hand me over to another man?"

His face scrunched as if he was in pain but then he straightened. "I'm only giving you choices."

She'd heard just about enough. Yanking her face from his hands, she scooted around him and stood. Completely naked, she glared at him with her hands on her hips. "You mean you don't want to be stuck with me."

"That isn't what I said at all. I don't want you to be stuck with me." He stood too and reached for her, but she jerked back.

"Don't touch me," she hissed. "Never touch me again." She spun, then fled the room to her own. It was only after she closed the door between them that she realized most of her clothing was still in his room. Not knowing what else to do, she burrowed into the cold bed, the fire having gone out hours before and pulled the covers over her head. Then, the tears started. He'd promised to marry her and he was going back on his word. She should have known better than to give herself over to a rake.

Grace should have known better than to take him at his word. Hadn't her mother warned her that her virtue was her greatest asset? Of course she knew her sisters and her cousins had broken that rule, but she wasn't them. Men adored them, found them deep, interesting, strong. She hiccupped. At least she did still have her maidenhead and if her family was here, her reputation might stay intact.

Everyone was always telling her to be kinder, more considerate, less selfish. Perhaps this was the lesson she needed. She'd be a better person and find a man who would love that woman. Tossing the covers back off her body, she rose in the freezing room, wrapping a blanket about herself and crossed back over to the connecting door.

She opened the door to find Ben exactly where she'd left him, his face in his hands. He looked up as the door clicked open and only then did she realize that she should have looked at her face first. It was likely red and puffy. "I forgot my clothes."

He stood and began collecting up the garments. "Your room must be freezing. I can feel the draft from here."

"It doesn't matter," she answered, straightening. She couldn't look into his eyes. "Don't worry about me."

He stopped in front of her and handed her the bundle of clothes. "As long as I live, I will worry about you, Lady Grace." Then he gently moved her and walked into her room. "Let me get the fire going. You start dressing in here."

She clutched the blanket tighter. He'd worry about her for as long as he lived? What did that mean?

BAD KNEW he'd upset her, but he wasn't entirely certain what he'd done wrong. Well, that was partially true. He'd dealt with women before. Emotional creatures the lot of them. He'd likely hurt her feelings but he'd done it for her own good.

She could and should have any man she wanted. He poked at the fire, getting a few of the coals to ignite the new wood he'd placed on the embers. Why should she have to settle for a scarred, socially inept barbarian of a man?

He pulled back the poker, realizing that he'd been jabbing the wood. Memories from the night before flooded his thoughts. He'd worshipped every part of her body as she'd bloomed underneath him. He might never be able to touch another woman again. She tasted sweeter, felt softer, hell, she even moaned at the exact pitch that sent his senses reeling. And then there were the times they weren't in bed. Even today, she challenged him, pushed him to be a better man. And he liked that about her. She was slowly but surely bringing out the best in him.

Her corset lay across the table and he picked the garment up, determined to set things right with Grace.

Walking to the connecting door, he softly knocked. "Grace, I have your corset."

The door cracked open and a hand reached through. Her long slender fingers opened and closed indicating for him to pass her the garment. He bent down and kissed the back of her fingers instead.

"Don't," she bit out.

He reached for her hand and slowly opened it again so that he might lay a kiss on her palm. "I think you misunderstood me earlier."

"I did not. You said you would marry me and then you withdrew your offer."

"No, that is not what I said." He reached for the door and pushed it open a bit wider. Grace now stood in her chemise and he tried not to frown in disappointment. No woman had ever looked so good naked. "What I said was if you wished to choose someone else, you still could. I didn't say I wouldn't marry you. I'm giving you the choice. That's all."

Silence met his words but her hand went limp in his. "You did say that, didn't you?"

"I'm not the likely choice for your hand, love." He brought her palm to his lips again. "Think that over before you decide."

She stepped closer to him, her head tilting up toward his. "Will you help me dress?"

"Of course," he answered. Truth be told, he wanted to strip her clothes back off and tuck her back into his bed.

Helping her put her clothes back on and then watching her dress her hair was a form of lovely torture. But when she was ready, he held out his elbow to take her down for breakfast. It was time to reunite her with her family.

His chest tightened as he forced his feet to move. He wanted to keep her all for himself.

CHAPTER ELEVEN

THEY ENTERED the common room and Grace looked around. She'd half expected various members of her family to be sitting in a row waiting for her.

But only a few stray guests sat about, drinking tea and eating biscuits. "What should we do?"

Bad gave her a sidelong glance. "Eat our breakfast."

She squeezed his arm. "You don't think we missed them, do you?"

He shook his head. "I heard them in what seemed to be the middle of the night. My guess is they're still in bed." Then he paused. "When we do find them, perhaps you shouldn't tell them that we already knew they were here. That might lead to questions."

Grace pressed her lips together. That was an excellent point. He escorted her to an empty table where a pot of tea was set in the middle. "What if they don't get up for hours? Do we continue to London as though we didn't know they were here?" she asked as she sat down. Had she managed to keep the hopeful note out of her voice?

"They're searching for you. I doubt they'll be much longer." He rubbed his chin.

She tapped the table. "Why didn't we run into Vice and Ada? You did say they were following you to my rescue."

His eyes widened. "That's an excellent question. We've been so busy, I forgot all about them."

They had been busy. A blush infused her cheeks. And tonight, whether they made it to London or were just travelling with her family, they'd have to sleep apart. She swallowed down a lump.

It wasn't just the fear. Though that most decidedly was a factor. It was also the feel of him. His muscles, his heat, the way he made her feel inside. She didn't want to be without him. "Do you think we'll reach London today?"

He shrugged. "Most likely."

She took a large sip of her tea then carefully set the cup down. "Where do you live in the city?"

He cocked his head to the side. "On Bradbury Street. Why?"

Her shoulders slumped. She didn't know it. "Where is that?" She wanted to know in case…well, in case she just couldn't be without him.

He cocked his eyebrows. "You know that you can't come traipsing to my house."

"I can if we're engaged," she sniffed. "Which we are."

He sat back in his chair. "It's your choice. I told you that. But don't make it too hastily. I don't want fear to be the reason you choose me."

She frowned. That was understandable. But she knew it wasn't why. "I am afraid but it's more than that."

"Well, I'll be," a man's voice boomed from the doorway. "We've found you after all." Lord Darlington crossed the room.

"Grace," her cousin, Minnie, squeaked behind him. "Thank goodness you're all right!"

Grace stood and embraced Minnie. A mixture of delight and regret assaulted her senses. While she was so glad to be reunited with her family, she'd miss her time alone with Ben. "I am. Thanks to Lord Baderness. He staged a very daring rescue."

"And Abernath?" Darlington asked.

Ben looked away. "Dead, I'm afraid."

Darlington gave a sharp nod. "I don't know if I should be happy or sad."

Grace shook her head. "She was sick in body and mind. I've seen it before. Pox all over her hands."

Minnie winced, hugging Grace again. "You poor thing."

Darlington put his arm around his wife. "And Crusher?"

"Also dead." Ben had moved closer and his hand came to Grace's back.

Daring stared at the two of them, missing nothing. "Did you see all of this transpire?"

She gave a tentative nod and Daring's face spasmed with regret. Ben let her go and leaned over to Daring. "She's having trouble sleeping."

That wasn't true. She would have trouble sleeping, except a certain man had kept her wrapped tight in his embrace. "I'll be all right."

"Grace," Diana called from the doorway rushing toward the group. "Thank the Lord." She threw her arms about Grace, who nearly fell back, but Ben caught her, propping them both back up.

Diana unwound her arms from Grace's neck and looked at Ben. "You're rather familiar."

Heat filled her cheeks at the truth in Diana's words. Diana always spoke her mind and with her dark hair and statuesque beauty, people usually listened. But Grace reached for her sister's hands. "I've made quite the nuisance of myself where Lord Baderness is concerned," she said. "I've been a bit jumpy and he's been very patient with my needs."

Diana frowned. "He hasn't taken advantage?"

Grace shook her head, not daring to look at Ben. "He's been a perfect gentleman."

Diana's shoulders relaxed. "And Abernath?"

Grace cringed. She hadn't been lying to the countess. Diana had felt a certain kinship with the woman. "She died, but don't be upset. She was ill and relieved for her death to be over so quickly and painlessly."

Diana stared at her sister. "Grace. Are you all right?"

Grace blinked. What did that mean? "Of course, I am. Don't I sound all right?"

"Yes. Very reasonable. Which is not…really…you."

Bad pressed his lips together to keep from laughing out loud. Diana had a way of putting a point on things.

When he thought about it, it wasn't dissimilar to Grace's manner and he quite liked it.

Grace, however, appeared less amused by Diana's comment. "Oh please," she said. "Just because you're married doesn't mean you can go around telling other people how to behave."

Lady Winthrop appeared in the doorway. "It would seem my daughter has been found and is unharmed. She's already putting her older sister in her place."

Grace gave a soft groan.

He leaned down. "Are you all right?"

Her lips pursed. "I'd rather face Abernath again."

"And you were rescued by a handsome lord. Tell me daughter, is there another wedding in our future?"

"Mother," Grace said. "Yes, I'm injured. A bit shaken still but managing to cope with the scare. Thanks for asking."

Ben nearly choked from the effort to suppress his chuckle. He was beginning to understand Grace in a whole new light. She came from a family of outspoken women who were also all uncommonly beautiful.

"Yes, yes," her mother answered as Lord Winthrop followed just behind his wife. "But still. The circumstances…"

Grace huffed a breath. "Lord Baderness should not be saddled with me simply because he was kind enough to rescue me."

Her father cleared his throat. "That will be my decision not yours. Baderness, I'd like a word."

He straightened, trying not to grimace. What was the man going to say? That Bad wasn't fit to be the carpet under his daughter's slippers? He might have a point, but it was going to hurt to hear it. "Of course, my lord."

The man turned back and Bad followed. But he hadn't made it a single step before a hand tugged at his arm. He looked back to see

Grace, her blue eyes staring up at him. "Don't let him strong-arm you."

He swallowed a lump of emotion. "I won't let him strong-arm *you*," he answered, then continued to follow. So strange, he'd lived his entire life alone. At least what he remembered. He supposed he'd had parents when he was very young, he just didn't remember them. After all this time, he hated to be apart from Grace.

Lord Winthrop led him into a private dining room and turned abruptly on heel. "You know what I wish to discuss?"

Bad swallowed the lump in his throat. "I have an idea."

Winthrop stepped closer. "Listen, son. Marriage doesn't have to change who you are."

Bad scrunched his brow. "I beg your pardon?"

Her father shifted. "If it's money you need, I've been spared three of my four daughters participating in society. There's extra."

"Extra?" He rubbed his face, trying to follow the thread of this conversation. "You aren't upset with me for being alone with your daughter?"

It was Winthrop's turn to look confused. "Upset? You saved her life. Right quickly too. But her reputation is at risk." He placed a hand on Bad's shoulder. "I know you came into the Barony unexpectedly. Grace would be an excellent match for you. Our bloodlines are impeccable and our social standing excellent. And you must have noticed that she's lovely. She'll make you beautiful babies."

Ben's stomach pitched and he nearly toppled over. A baby. His baby. He imagined Grace round with his child and his heart nearly stopped in his chest. "She would." His voice was raspy and he barely found the air to push them out.

Her father nodded eagerly. "You'd be helping her. And in return, we'd help you."

Bad cleared his throat, trying to calm his body. "I agree with all you've said."

"Good." He slapped Bad's arm. "It's agreed."

But Bad raised his other hand. "It's not me I'm concerned about.

It's Grace. As you said, I was not meant for the title. I wasn't raised for it." That was an understatement.

Her father shrugged. "You've got one now. And a woman like my daughter would aid your success."

Winthrop was likely right. "Don't you think Grace could have a duke or a marquess? Do you really want her to settle for a baron?"

The man squinted. "Becoming a baroness is far superior to being a spinster."

Bad nodded. "I agree. And I won't let that happen to her, but I wanted to give her a choice of husbands before she's saddled with me."

Her father frowned. "I'll not pay for a season, knowing that a secret like this could ruin her at any moment." The man stood straighter, still tall and fairly broad.

Bad said a silent prayer that Winthrop wasn't planning violence, holding up his hands.

"I didn't want to have to start your relationship like this but I'll force the issue if I have to," her father said.

Bad frowned. "I've already informed Grace that I will marry her."

The man instantly relaxed, smiling at Bad. "Good. Perfect. Then there's no need to continue this conversation."

"I disagree," Bad answered. "Take whatever extra money you were going to give me and use it for Grace to participate in this year's season. If at any point people believe she's ruined, we'll marry. But give her a chance to find someone better."

His heart cracked in his chest. Part of him wanting to take all those words back, agree with her father's plan, and marry Grace at the earliest possible moment. She could be his.

Like lightning his feelings penetrated his mind. He was in love with her. He'd seen his friends fall one by one and yet he hadn't recognized the symptoms himself. His inability to be without her, the way every part of her was appealing.

Her father grunted. "You're willing to be the backup plan?"

"For her? Yes." His heart stuttered again. In between the beats it cried that he was making a terrible mistake.

"I'm not sure I can support that, but I'll think on it for a day."

He gave a nod, ignoring his own pain. This was for her.

CHAPTER TWELVE

GRACE LOOKED at the door for what had to have been the tenth time in the last three minutes. She was surrounded by people who loved her and would protect her no matter what, but she didn't feel right without Ben.

Which only reaffirmed what she already knew. Her attachment to him was about a great deal more than safety.

Not that she didn't know that, but still, every time he was away, it reaffirmed her feelings.

She took another sip of tea, her eyes sliding to the door again.

"Grace," Emily chirped from her right, having joined the group a few moments prior. "Do you want to ride in our carriage?" Her eldest sister dropped her voice. "We all know how mother will be."

Her heart began to thud wildly. She'd be separated from Ben the entire day too? Why hadn't she thought of that? "I can sit with Lord Baderness. I'd hate to leave him with Crusher's carriage."

"Don't be silly," her mother answered. "You can't ride with him, dear."

Grace clenched her fist under the table. She'd been alone with him for nearly two days. It was on the tip of her tongue to say that they were engaged. But once she did that…

She didn't hold back for her sake. She'd happily marry him tomorrow. Grace held back her words for him. "Mother," she set her cup down, staring just over her mother's shoulder, careful to not look her in the eye. "I may never ask this question again." She swallowed, her insides churning. "But how could I improve myself? Be a better person."

Diana drew in a sharp breath while Emily dropped her spoon in her tea, causing it to splash. Her mother stared for a moment before she reached for her hand. "Since you've asked, I—"

"No," Minnie stopped her aunt before she could begin. "Grace. Why are you asking this?"

Heat flushed her cheeks as she twisted her hands. "Sometimes I wish that I was more like Cordelia or Diana or you, Minnie." Her only known talent was beauty while Cordelia was so smart and Minnie terribly brave and strong. What did they say about her? Spoiled.

Minnie frowned, her brows drawing together. "Everyone sees the best of others and wishes to be more like those people." Minnie leaned closer. "But you're wonderful, Grace."

Grace shook her head. "I know what you all think. I act selfishly, I speak without thinking, I—"

"Grace," Diana soothed, her voice soft and gentle. "I speak without thinking. You speak with pointed accuracy."

Grace shook her head. "I'm not bold."

Emily grabbed her hand. "But you're strong. Look at how you're holding up in the face of all this insanity. What makes you think you need to change?"

She drew in a deep breath. "He's attracted to me, but he doesn't like me." She gazed at her lap.

No one spoke, silence stretching out between them until finally Diana cleared her throat. "I have no idea if that's true or not but I can tell you that the right man for you will like you exactly as you are. Do not change yourself for his benefit. That will not make you happy."

Grace didn't look up. "But I like him. In fact…" Did she dare to say the words out loud?

"In fact, what?" Minnie scooted closer.

"I think that I love him." Grace nibbled her lip.

Diana cleared her throat again. "Is it possible that you're just grateful for his rescue?"

She shook her head. "I don't think so. I felt this even before the kidnapping. This growing need to be near him all the time."

Minnie raised her brows. "But the two of you argued constantly."

Grace shrugged, finally looking up from her lap. "There was this energy between us and I didn't know what to do with it so I would just tease him. I—"

Emily grabbed her hand. "Heaven help us, you are in love."

"What do you think he and Papa are discussing?" Grace asked as the other women shifted.

"Your marriage, of course," her mother answered. "He's been alone with you."

Grace drew in a deep breath. "Then I've no choice but to change. I love him, we're going to marry. I can't bear to have these feelings and not have them returned." She drew in a shaky breath. "He says that he wants me to have options, but he's been trying to get out of our union. What else am I supposed to think?"

Her family was silent. There was nothing to say. She was woefully correct.

BAD WALKED BACK into the common room to find the women huddled together, their heads bent, but no one spoke a word. Silent women were the worst sort because it wasn't natural and therefore meant something had gone very wrong.

And right now, he knew what the problem was: him.

Had she told them what he'd done last night? Or had she shared his past? How he was a former poor orphan trying to bed a lady.

His insides tightened and he let out a soft groan. Grace's eyes snapped to his and she stood so quickly her chair fell back, crashing to the floor.

The noise made the other women jump and Grace cried out, her eyes wide. He was at her side in an instant, righting the chair. "There's no cause for concern," he said, in a hushed voice that was meant to soothe.

"We were discussing which carriage I should ride back to London in, my mother's or Jack and Emily's. I…" She looked up at him, her lip trembling.

"We can't go back to London yet," Diana interrupted. "We need to collect Lady Abernath's body."

"I beg your pardon," Lady Winthrop inserted. "We do not."

Diana held up her hand. "Listen. We're going to say we all came out here because of what Crusher did to Abernath. Then we're going to give her a proper burial. Not only does it serve us, but it helps Harry. And…" Diana paused. "The woman was ill and a victim in her own way. She doesn't deserve a delinquent's grave."

Grace moved closer to Ben. Not only did this plan delay their return to London, it gave her more time with him. "I agree. It's a solid plan."

Lady Winthrop stood. "You can't be serious. The woman stole two of my daughters and I haven't the first clue why. Feel sorry for her? And why is your sister Cordelia raising her child? I want answers."

Grace took another partial step toward him, her shoulder brushing his chest. Whatever had made the women quiet, they were over it now and he realized he'd like their silence back because these questions were going to crush him.

He brushed her back with his fingers, trying to give Grace the comfort she craved. Minnie and Diana both stared and he pulled back his fingers. They were two of the most intimidating women he knew. Together, they may very well swallow him whole.

"Lady Winthrop." Daring approached the table. "I think it best that I explain. But first, I'd like a word with my friend, if you'd permit me." Then he looked at Bad.

Bad let out an audible sigh. Again? "Of course," he answered, his fingers brushing Grace's back once again. She pressed closer.

"Lady Winthrop, can Grace accompany us as well? We'll only go to the other room."

Grace's mother waved her hand. "By all means. Why should any of us stand on ceremony or follow a single social rule? I raised you girls correctly. What's happened?"

Daring gave Lady Winthrop a wink. "They ran into a gaggle of scandalous lords, my lady. But fear not. They've done an admirable job of taming the lot of us." He cleared his throat. "And that includes Grace."

Grace shook her head. "Oh no, I haven't—"

Daring held up his hand. "Baderness, are you or are you not going to marry Grace?"

Bad straightened but he didn't take his hand off her back. "I am hers if she wants me."

A ripple of whispers went through the women.

He tightened his hand at her waist. "But Grace deserves a season. So, I am going to wait to make sure I'm her first choice."

The whispers rose to a roar.

"A season?"

"Why not marry now?"

"What if you're ruined?" The jumble of her family's voices were too loud to hear who was saying what.

They continued on and he honestly couldn't tell who said what.

Grace opened her mouth, her hand lifting to his chest. But before she could speak, Daring did.

"In that case." He turned to Lady Winthrop, "I was once engaged to Lady Abernath. She threatened to expose an old secret and kidnapped the girls as a form of leverage to get me to confess."

Lady Winthrop gripped the table. "Why didn't I learn of this before?"

"We've only just figured it out, Mother." Grace answered. "She confessed to me in the carriage on the way here."

"What's the secret? Will it ruin all of us?"

"No." Daring held out his hands. "It's of no consequence. The woman was going mad, losing her mental faculties."

Bad knew that wasn't entirely true and that Grace was protecting him, Daring, and their club in saying so. He wanted to pull her in his arms. He wanted to give her everything that was his to give.

Daring gave a quick nod. "Lord Effington, Lord Baderness, and myself will retrieve the body. Lord Exmouth will return the rest of you to London. We'll be back by tomorrow midday."

Grace trembled. A palpable shake that reverberated through him. "I'd prefer to travel with the ladies. After what's happened, they might need protection," Bad said.

Daring raised his brows but he gave a nod of assent. "Fair enough. I trust your judgment."

Grace nearly melted into Bad. He closed his eyes, knowing they'd marry. He wanted her to have a season, it was the best choice for her long term, but right now, she needed him too much and she'd ruin herself if she acted this way in front of anyone other than her family. He'd get a lovely wife if she did that, but her? He held her tighter. He truly wanted what was best for her now and in the future.

CHAPTER THIRTEEN

Grace tapped her foot as they rode in the carriage. She knew that Ben was on the seat with the driver of the carriage, just feet away, but she wanted to be next to him.

"Grace," Diana chided. "You've barely listened to a word."

"You don't know that," she answered, looking out the window.

"Don't mind her," Lady Winthrop added. "She's in love and lost in her thoughts."

Grace's lips pressed together. She'd admitted the words out loud so she couldn't deny them but… "I've already told you. It's the possibility of not having my feelings returned that has me in fits."

Diana shook her head. "We all felt that way at some point. Try to understand, you're both new to each other and it can be difficult to admit how you feel because you're not sure if the other will reject you. You'll hold back and so will he." Diana reached for her hand. "But he cares for you as much as you do him. It's in his every movement, the way he touches you, the expression on his face." She squeezed Grace's fingers lightly. "Stop worrying. And if you really want to hear him say how he feels, tell him first."

Grace shook her head. It couldn't actually be that simple, could it? But those words stuck with her as they drove back into London. They turned over in her thoughts as they reached their London townhome and pulled through the iron gates.

As she stepped out of the carriage, her home looked exactly the same but everything was different. She'd been kidnapped, saved, and had fallen in love.

Turning back to the carriage, she watched Bad climb down from the seat, his muscles flexing with his movement. She held her breath as he swiveled to face her and then took the three steps to be at her side. The day had warmed nicely and the sun shone down on her face.

Leaning close to him, she whispered, "Meet me at the gate to the left at midnight."

His eyes widened but he gave a quick jerk of his chin. "It will be cool tonight. Dress warmly."

Her mother approached and Grace took a quick step back. Some of the tension she'd felt eased.

"Lord Baderness," her mother called. "Won't you join us for dinner?"

"I'd be delighted," he answered, taking Grace's hand and bringing her gloved fingers to his lips.

Grace beamed at her mother. For once, their purposes aligned. Her mother winked back.

After saying their goodbyes, Grace watched as both Ben and her sisters left. Turning back to the house with both her parents, she realized how empty the space had become. "What will you do when we're all gone?" she asked her mother as she stepped through the entry.

Her mother gave her a glowing smile. "Each of your sisters' husbands has a residence in London. I fully expect to see this place filled with children regularly. And…" Her mother's smile broadened into a wide grin. "I won't have to worry nearly so much. As a grandmother, I'll be free to just love my grandchildren."

Grace cocked her head to the side. Her mother had driven her near mad at times, but she'd never considered how difficult being the mother of four daughters might be. "You've done a wonderful job. Well, I suppose I might be the exception, but all my sisters have married well."

Her mother shook her head. "Look at you, my Grace. Growing into a thoughtful and mature woman. You'll do marvelously. Don't you doubt that."

Grace thanked her mother and headed up the stairs for a bath and, perhaps, a nap. A rosy glow filled her as she considered how little sleep she'd gotten the night before. Completely worth the trouble.

Soaking in a long bath, she climbed out of the tub and allowed herself to dry, then put on a night rail to rest before the evening. Her eyes were heavy as the afternoon sun streamed in.

Grace wasn't certain how much time had passed but a dream woke her. In it, she was being held by Crusher. Ben tried to save her, but he moved further and further away. She struggled and pulled, trying to reach him, but the more she tried, the smaller he became until he disappeared from view.

She woke in a panic, the sun gone and the room cast in darkening shadows. Wiping the sweat from her brow, she sat up. She had to find a way to sleep in his arms tonight. She didn't wish to be alone.

Rising from the bed, she pulled the cord to call for a servant to help her dress. The dream was about her fear from the kidnapping but it was more than that. She was desperately afraid she'd lose Ben after she'd only just found him. Diana was right. It was time to tell him how she felt.

An hour and half later, she stood at the top of the stairs in one of her favorite gowns made of blue silk. It swept off her shoulders and cinched just below her bosom, highlighting the ample curve of her bustline. She pulled her hair back into a soft coif at her nape, allowing a few artful pieces to dance about her neck and shoulders.

She pressed her hands to her midriff, hoping that she looked pretty enough for what she was about to do.

Glancing down the stairs, she saw Ben standing with Exile in the foyer just as Daring and Effing came through the doors.

"It's done," Daring's voice boomed up the stairs. "We've brought her back to London and made arrangements for a proper funeral."

Ben looked to his friend and didn't see her at the top of the steps, which worked fine for her. It gave her a moment to drink in the details of his face, the lines of his body, her own responding to the very sight of him. She smoothed her skirts as she started down the stairs.

"Good," Ben answered, still not seeing her. "I'm glad to know that Harry will be protected from this scandal. If we've done one thing right, it's made that boy safe."

Effing nodded. "When we sell the club, we'll use the proceeds to fund his earldom. We're all financially stable now, we don't need the money."

"Agreed," Exile grunted. "Sin can oversee the transfer. In the meantime, we'll have to decide upon a way to discreetly vet possible buyers."

Grace's brow furrowed. Did Ben really wish to sell the club? But she didn't need to ask as Effing did it for her. "Bad, how do you feel about letting the club go? You spent more time there than any of us."

She stopped, nearly at the bottom of the steps as her heart raced in her chest. She wasn't certain she wanted to hear his answer, in fact her stomach pitched with nerves but she couldn't make her voice work to announce her presence either.

"I don't have much choice in the matter," he rumbled, his eyes casting to the floor.

What did that mean? Nausea made her head spin and she covered her mouth with her hand. If there was one thing she didn't want to do, it was force him into a match that Ben didn't want. "I beg to differ," she said, announcing her presence. "You have all the choice in the world."

DREAD MADE Bad's stomach drop. He hadn't meant the words the way they sounded. He wanted nothing more than to marry her. The club, however, was a part of his past. First, all his partners had married. He didn't want to run the place without them. Second, somewhere over the past few months he'd outgrown the place.

He no longer wished to spend his time with drunk and rowdy

men. It occurred to him that in some ways, he'd recreated his past in his present. Sure, he had more money, but still, he dealt with the basest facets of humanity.

He touched the ring rattling in his pocket. He'd bought it this morning because…well mostly because he couldn't stop thinking about her. But also Bad wanted to be prepared. If Grace were ruined, their marriage would be swift to ensure she was protected as much as possible.

He drank in the sight of Grace standing before him in that dress… God, she made a man ache for more. She looked so lovely—soft, tempting, stunning—standing there. And she appeared…hurt. "Grace." He reached out to her. "I only meant that with all my partners retiring—"

She held up her hand, her shoulders squaring as she descended the last few steps. The men parted for her and she stepped in front of him. "It's all right. You don't have to placate me. I need to tell you something."

"What?" His chest tightened as he looked down at her determined face.

That sweet pink tongue darted out to lick her lips. "I…"

She drew in a deep breath, more pink spreading across her cheeks. She was perfection.

"I love you," she said.

His mouth dropped open and his breath stuck in his throat. "What?"

She pressed her hands to her stomach. "I love you and I want what's best for you and—"

"Grace." He reached for her waist. "You don't have to say that." She wanted his protection and he knew that even if she didn't.

The men around him shifted.

She put a hand to his chest. He wasn't certain if she was going to pull him closer or push him away. "I'm not just saying that. This afternoon I fell asleep and had a nightmare about Crusher."

He nodded. "I know, love. You want to be near me because you're afraid. But your fear will fade and then you'll be stuck with me."

She shook her head, pulling him closer. "I want to be stuck with you. What made me afraid in the dream was that you kept getting further and further away from me. The harder I tried to pull you closer, the more distance grew between us." She drew in a breath. "I love you and so I am going to let you go." Her palms spread out on his jacket.

"Let me go?" He tightened his hands on her waist. Did she actually love him? Was it just her fear speaking for her? "But your father. He—"

"Let me worry about him." She patted his chest with her palm. "Though, you might consider leaving London for a while." She bit her lip. "But I will not tie you to me just because you rescued me. I don't think either of us will be happy then."

His heart was racing in his chest. "Why wouldn't you be happy?"

Her gaze cast down to the floor. "I told you. I love you. I can't be married to you knowing how I feel and understanding that you don't feel the same. That I am just an obligation to you."

Words crowded in his mouth but they stuck there, not coming out. She was letting him go because she loved him. Did she really feel that way or was it just his protection she craved?

"For crying out loud, would you kiss her already?" Exile groaned from next to him. "You've left the poor girl hanging."

CHAPTER FOURTEEN

GRACE RESISTED the urge to nibble at her lip as tension built inside her. She gripped his shirt tighter as he opened his mouth. "Just so we're clear. You think you love me?"

Her fingers loosened in his shirt and she gave him a tiny push. "No, that's not what I said."

He shook his head, his features tense. "Grace. Love. I know that you feel an attachment to me now, but I also know that there are better men out there." Ones that were worthy of her love. Hell, not even his own family had loved him. They hadn't cared enough to pull him from the streets. Why should Grace be any different?

She gave his chest a light smack. "You weren't listening to me. I told you. It wasn't Crusher I was afraid of in my dream, it was losing you." Then she smacked at his chest again, this time harder. "I love you despite the fact that you are annoyingly hardheaded and unwillingly to see what is right in front of your face."

The men around them chuckled and someone called. "She's got you there."

He smiled too. "Try to understand. No one in my entire life has actually loved me. At least not that I can remember. Even if I knew how, I always assumed that no one had ever cared because I wasn't worth caring for."

Grace's heart roared in her ears. His comments about being a street urchin rang through her thoughts. All this time, she'd thought that she wasn't good enough but he felt that way about himself too.

Pushing up on her toes, she touched the tip of her nose to his, her fingers gliding up the collar of his shirt to his exposed neck. "Not good enough?" Her breath caught as she tilted her chin to better gaze into his eyes. "You are the best man I've ever met in my life. I can only hope to make myself worthy of your affection."

"For Christ's sake," Darlington groaned. "You're a big giant oaf."

A shadow of a grin turned Ben's lips up. "Make yourself worthy?" Then he leaned in and softly kissed her lips. The touch so gentle, she ached with need. "You, my lovely Grace, are my queen. I'll have to throw myself at your feet daily and beg you to love me."

Then, before she could respond and tell him that was hardly necessary, he kissed her again. This time it wasn't gentle, this time the press of his mouth demanded passion and she met his need with all her own.

She forgot about the men around her, the fact that her parents could arrive at any moment, the details of their engagement or lack thereof. All she could feel was him and she never wanted this kiss to end.

But all too soon, he lifted his head and cupping her face in his hands, whispered in her ear. "We're still meeting at the gate at midnight."

"Yes," she replied, though it hadn't really been a question.

"And tonight, we'll announce our intentions to marry." He kissed her cheek, brushing back a strand of her hair.

She nodded, joy bursting inside her. But then he did something she hadn't expected. Dropping to one knee, he slid his hands down her arms, grasping her gloved fingers in his own. "Grace." His voice had risen, echoing about the entry.

She heard a gasp from above and looked up to see her mother and sister standing above. How long had they been there?

"Yes?" she said just above a breathy whisper.

He gave her fingers a squeeze before he let them go to reach into his pocket. From the inside of his coat he pulled a small silk satchel and slid open the string. Tipping the bag, a ring toppled onto the palm of his hand.

She gasped as the blue stone caught the candlelight, sparkling in the night. But closing the ring in his palm, he began to unbutton the glove of her left hand. "Would you, Lady Grace, do me the honor of becoming my wife?" Then, finger by finger, he tugged off her glove, exposing her hand underneath.

"Yes," she answered, tears filling her eyes.

Grasping the sparkling sapphire cut in a rectangle shape and encrusted with diamonds, he slid the piece onto her finger. "We'll have it fitted soon." He grimaced as he assessed the size. "I bought it today for just such an event as this."

She shook her head, her mouth hanging open. "You bought me an engagement ring today?"

"Well, I wanted to be prepared."

She swatted his hand with her now-ringed one. "I just put my heart on a platter for you and all your friends to see and you were planning on proposing anyway?"

He drew his brows together. "I'd already proposed. Remember?"

"But..." she started.

"Grace," Ben interrupted. "You know I love our bits of banter. I have loved you since the first moment I saw you, and as I've gotten to know you, my feelings have only strengthened. I bought the ring because I wanted to be prepared for the event that you might possibly return my feelings."

"Oh," she answered, heat filling her cheeks. That was actually lovely.

"Well, I'll be," her mother called from above. "My daughter is getting married."

"Yes." Grace didn't look up, but instead, looked right at Ben. "I am."

BEN REFUSED to let go of her hand. Even as her mother and Emily hugged her, even when her father came down, beaming and, slapping him on the arm, said they needed to have another chat.

Grace was his. How the fates had aligned to allow him such a wife as her, he had no idea but he didn't think he'd let her out of his sight for even a moment until after the wedding. Perhaps not even for some time after the blessed event.

He should have used the word love too. Grace had. As she'd said. She'd offered her heart on a platter. He tightened his grip on her hand as if that would keep her at his side.

"Let's all go to dinner," her mother chirped. "We've got so much to discuss."

Bad shrugged, keeping Grace's hand in his. He hadn't returned her glove. He rather liked looking down at her delicate fingers clasped in his as the ring he'd just given her sparkled back up at him. Just like a queen, he thought he might drape her in jewels. Her skin was the perfect palette to watch them glimmer in the moonlight.

"We'll need to get you a necklace to match," he murmured close to her ear.

She frowned, looking over at him. "You won't have the club anymore. Perhaps jewels are not the best use of money."

He raised his brows. He'd done well for himself over the years, building up a fortune that dukes would envy. He'd stayed with the club because he'd felt at home there long after his financial worries had vanished. "I'll never leave you uncared for, Grace." His eyebrows lifted. "But is the girl who insisted on shopping for ribbon the same one who now cautions me against purchasing her pretty baubles?"

She sniffed, trying to hold back a grin but not quite succeeding. "That's when I thought I needed a husband. Now I have one."

He laughed then. He'd never tire of her wit. In fact, he was certain it was part of what would keep him entertained for years. "Well, just so you know, I meant what I said about attending you like my queen." He dropped his head down to place a soft kiss on her neck.

She turned her head to rub her cheek against his. "I can think of a few better ways for you to worship me."

Heat and desire that had been simmering just below the surface, roared up inside him. "I can barely wait."

"Grace," Lady Winthrop called from the front of the group. "When do you think you'd like to have the wedding? Perhaps a month from now? That should give us time to properly plan."

He stopped and Grace's fingers tightened in his. "A month?"

"Six weeks, perhaps?" her mother asked. "That will give us time to post the banns and…"

Her father interrupted. "I'd prefer sooner. We do have a scandal nipping at our heels."

Bad's insides relaxed a bit, his shoulders drooping.

But then her father continued. "Perhaps a fortnight?"

Her mother clucked her tongue. "Can't one of my daughters have a proper wedding? I haven't been able to plan a single one. Not really."

Grace shook her head as Bad tightened a hand about her waist. He knew Grace would prefer to spend her nights in his bed and he had a powerful need to keep her by his side. "My lord," he started. "Perhaps something even sooner. We don't want—"

"No." Her mother waved her hand. "This is my last chance."

"Mother," Grace interjected. "After everything that's happened, it seems wise to have a quick engagement."

Her mother stopped, planting her hands on her hips. She looked very much like Grace in that moment. "A fortnight is ridiculously fast."

Grace clamped her mouth shut but Ben noted the jaunty set to her jaw. He'd seen that look before and when Grace gave it, she usually got her way.

Daring turned back to him then, having been unusually quiet. "Grace," the duke rumbled. "May I borrow your fiancé for just a moment?"

Grace frowned but slipped her hand from his. "Of course." Then she moved ahead, joining her mother who'd begun to discuss churches and spring flowers, and which dress most suited the occasion.

"What is it?" Bad asked, his voice dropping low. He didn't much like the interruption and he didn't care if Daring knew it.

Daring stopped, reaching for Bad's arm. "I've a ship leaving in the wee hours of the morning."

"What?"

"It's headed to Scotland. I've a winter crop of barley to deliver and cases of whisky to return. Rather close to Gretna Green, all things considered."

Bad scrubbed his jaw with his hand. "A ship you say?" Daring might be his new best friend in all of the world. "Leaving tomorrow?"

"Four or so, as the tide flows." Daring slapped him on the back. "If I'm not mistaken, Malice and Cordelia should be reaching Scotland to see his family on their wedding tour. Perhaps they could be coerced into stopping in Gretna Green as well."

That confused him a bit. "They're already married."

Daring shook his head. "A woman likes to have a little family in attendance."

Bad looked up to where Grace stood next to her mother, the other woman still talking without pause. Would Grace elope with him?

He knew she would, but his chest tightened again. Should she? He was still a man who didn't know how to express himself. She'd offered her heart on a platter and he'd yet to even confess his love. He'd said he'd worship her but this was different. His heart twisted again. He couldn't let her go, they'd marry for certain. But he'd need to learn how to share his feelings to keep her forever.

CHAPTER FIFTEEN

Grace stood by the garden gate, trying to hold still. The truth was, she was excited. The man she was going to marry, who had proposed in front of all of her family, was meeting her in a dark garden at midnight.

She tightened her grip on the wrought iron gate. He was the man who'd already made her body sing. Would he touch her again tonight? Her insides fluttered as she peered into the darkness.

Her mother had talked of nothing but wedding plans until Grace had cried headache and retired for the evening. The truth was, she couldn't care less how they married, she was far more concerned with when.

Besides her fear after the kidnapping, she no longer liked being without him and the weeks, or if her mother had her way, months, until their ceremony would be torture. After the intimacy they'd shared, she couldn't go back to sleeping alone for too long.

The sound of gravel crunching stopped her thoughts and she ducked behind the brick post checking to make certain it was Ben who was coming down the path to the gate.

He was nearly at the fence when she finally saw him and popped up from her hiding spot. "Ben." She raced for the latch and clicked it open, backing up to make room for him to come through. He was in the garden in a second and swept her into his arms as the gate clanged closed behind him.

"Oh dear," she whispered, peeking over his shoulder even as her arms wrapped about his neck. "That was loud."

He grinned, kissing the hollow of her neck. "If we're caught, your mother will cease talking about our wedding that's to happen in two months' time."

Tension skittered along her skin. "I can't wait that long. Can you?"

"Gads, no," he rumbled as his lips kissed a trail to just behind her ear. "I think we both know I am not a man who stands on convention."

A little gasping giggle erupted from her lips. It was funny and true and he was tickling the sensitive skin or her earlobe. "I'm not sure how to convince my mother otherwise. She seems rather determined. I think she feels cheated out of a proper wedding."

"Is there a back stair where we can go to your room? It's even chillier out here than I thought it would be and I have some things to discuss with you."

"Discuss?" she asked just a touch of fear sliding down her spine that tinged with regret. She wanted so much more than a little chat.

He nipped along her jaw, finding her lips and giving them a long, lingering kiss. "About how we're going to circumvent your mother."

Her fingers wound into his hair. "Oh. Yes. That's a good idea." Then she kissed him again, long and slow, opening her mouth and sliding her tongue along his bottom lip. She'd already forgotten about going inside. She rather liked being out here in the dark, cool night.

She hardly noticed he'd begun moving until they were at the back door and he set her down.

Grabbing her hand, he twisted the knob and peeked his head in. "It's clear," he whispered as he pulled her inside and softly closed the door behind them. "Which way?"

She led him up the servant's stairs to the second floor and into her room. "We could have stayed outside. I was warm next to you."

He gave her a soft glance, the sort that relaxed the muscles of his face. "We'll be far more comfortable sleeping in a bed."

At that, she tossed her arms about his neck. "I'm so glad to sleep in your arms." Perhaps coming inside was an excellent idea after all. She should have learned by now that following him almost always worked to her advantage.

"I know it quiets your fears," he whispered, his voice gathering a hoarseness that hadn't been there before.

"It's more than that," she said as he clicked the door closed behind them. "I find that I am happiest in your arms."

He stilled. "I pray you always feel that way."

"Why wouldn't I?" she asked leaning back. "Are you still afraid I'll find you lacking? I love you exactly as you are."

His hands came to her hair, brushing the strands back from her face. "How did I get so lucky as to claim you for my own?"

———

BAD'S CHEST tightened as he looked down into her lovely blue-eyed gaze.

She gave him a soft smile. "You're lucky?" Her head shook between his hands. "You saved me, remember? I'm fairly certain all the pleasure has been mine."

His own body tightened at her reference. "I got an immense amount of pleasure out of our night together."

One of her brows quirked up. "Is that so?" She slid her palms down his chest. "Explain that to me. I want to know."

His eyes closed for a moment. His cock had hardened just thinking about touching her. Now she wanted him to say it out loud? "Men are not so complicated as women. Looking at and touching a woman's body makes us very excited."

Her fingers continued skimming down his stomach and over his waist then further until she reached the head of his manhood, thick with desire. "Oh," she gasped, exploring his man parts with tentative strokes. "Are they always this…large?"

He chuckled then even as his cock swelled bigger. "No. And I'm glad for you to know that fact. I can only hope it's one of my qualities that keeps you interested."

She gave him a firmer squeeze and a rumble of pleasure rattled in his chest. "Enough of that nonsense." Her hand dipped lower, holding his sac. "I already told you that I am yours forever. You're stuck with me. Soon it will be for better and for worse."

His brain began to buzz and he drew in a deep breath, attempting to clear his thoughts. "That is what I wanted to discuss. There is a ship bound for Scotland tomorrow."

"Scotland?" Her hand dropped to her side and he grimaced in regret. "Go to Scotland?"

Burying his fingers in her hair at the base of her skull, he tipped her head back. "We could marry tomorrow or the next day." He should tell her that he loved her or at the very least explain that he had a desperate need to tie her to him in some irreversible way. Despite the words of love falling from her lips, he still feared she'd change her mind.

"Yes," she answered and then stood on tiptoe to place her lips under his again. "Yes, I'll go to Scotland with you. Where you go, I follow."

His breath caught in his throat and he could barely speak as he stared down at her again. "Grace." The single word tightened his chest. "Love."

She smiled at him. "You've been calling me your love for a while now. Is that a term you always use?"

He blinked. When had he started that? "No. Never. I didn't even realize—"

"Show me." She kissed him again. "Show me the ways you love me." Then she reached for his cock again.

Bloody hell and damnation, now was the moment that he should not just call her love but tell her that he loved her absolutely and completely. But his throat wouldn't work and so instead, he picked her up and carried her to the bed.

She was already in a state of partial undress and he thanked his lucky stars for that as he fumbled with the buttons at her front. When he pulled back the garment to reveal her bare breasts, he groaned aloud and dropped his mouth to first the right and then the left. She moaned underneath him, arching up to meet his mouth.

Her response calmed him and his fingers slowed as he pulled the fabric further off her body then shrugged out of his coat.

"Ben," she murmured, reaching her arms up to him.

Love and desire coursed through him. "Would you undo your hair for me, love?"

He kept pulling off his clothes and she sat up and unlaced the braid that hung down her back. As her hair fell loose about her shoulders, he moved closer. He only wore his breeches now and he had the powerful urge to strip her of the rest of her clothes but first, he wanted to run his hands through that glorious mane of hair.

It slipped through his fingers, like fine silk or water from the river. She sat on the bed in front of him as he stood over her, looking down at the waves of golden strands flowing down her back. "Beautiful."

She brought her hands to his bare stomach, tracing the ridges of muscles that disappeared below the falls of his breeches. "I might say the same."

"My muscles will disappear eventually."

She shrugged. "My hair will turn grey. I will promise to want you always if you are willing to do the same for me."

He blinked. "I promise." Then he leaned down and kissed her. Somehow, the thought of watching her grow old, turn grey, didn't frighten him. In fact, it clogged his chest with emotion. "I would love nothing more than to spend my life growing old with you, Grace." He swallowed. "I love you with every bit of my heart."

She gave him a glowing smile. "I love you too."

CHAPTER SIXTEEN

GRACE TRIED to breathe but his words had stolen the air from her lungs. Joy swept through her.

Cupping her cheeks, he bent even lower. "If you let me, I will spend my life worshipping you, my queen."

And then he pushed her back on the bed and they fell together, lips touching, chests pressed heart to heart, pelvises in perfect alignment. Her breath caught as one of his hands slipped up her bare leg under her skirt. Skimming the back of her knee, he brushed the sensitive skin of her thigh making her quiver with need.

But when the tips of his fingers brushed between her legs, pleasure zipped through her entire body and she pressed against him silently begging him for more.

He answered with the same silence, his fingers doing all the talking as they started a gentle, leisurely rhythm over her sensitive flesh.

She clung to his back as her body tightened with growing need. When she thought she couldn't stand another moment, he stopped. Groaning in frustration, she lifted her head. "Please."

He responded by kissing her long and deep. "I want your clothes off."

With trembling fingers, she pulled at the garments but he brushed her hands away and completed the task himself.

He skimmed his hands from her neck, down her chest, over her stomach and along her hips, tracing her legs clear down to her toes. When he reached them, he bent down and placed a light kiss on her instep. "You are perfection."

She propped on her elbows, to stare down at him. "I can assure you, you are the only person who thinks that."

He kissed up her calf, nipping at the skin just behind her knee. Her body convulsed in a shiver. "They haven't seen you like this."

That made her eyebrows lift. "That's true." But she couldn't say more as his lips traversed her thigh. Her core was tightening with an ache and she bit her lip to keep from begging again.

Just before her sex, he stopped, drawing in a deep breath. "Your smell," he whispered. "Your taste…" The he licked her swollen lower lips.

She gasped and then moaned, her body wracked with a shiver as her hands dug into his hair.

"Perfect," he said as he pulled away for a moment and then leaned back in to kiss her again.

Tension was tightening inside her, the ache so keen, she thought she might die from pleasure. "Perhaps," she gasped. "I am only perfect for you."

He stopped then, his tongue stilling and this time she moaned again but not from pleasure, rather from frustration. "That is an interesting point. Someone else may not find your scent so pleasing or—"

"Ben." She dug her fingers deep into his scalp even as she pulled at his hair. "Do I have to beg?"

He gave her a slow grin. "I think that sounds lovely." Then the grin turned wicked. "But I like it equally well when you demand."

Her heel dug into the small of his back. "Very well. I demand that you finish what you've started."

"I changed my mind. Beg."

In answer, she pushed harder, squeezing with her thighs. He

laughed, his breath tickling her sensitive skin. "That's my girl," he said and then kissed her again.

Waves of pleasure rocked her body as he inserted a finger deep inside her channel and suddenly she was tipping over the edge falling into an abyss. She might have been frightened but he held her hips in his hands, solid despite the sensation spinning her out of control.

As she floated back to reality, he was gone but only for a moment. When he came back, his chest pressed to hers, his legs settling in the open juncture of her thighs, the hard press of his manhood parting her tender and swollen flesh. "Grace," he ground out between his teeth.

In response, she wrapped her arms about his neck, looking up into his eyes. "I'm ready for you."

―――

NEED PULSED THROUGH BAD, making thought near impossible. He'd wanted to wait. But in this moment, he couldn't stand another moment without making her his.

Grace was meant to be here with him, skin to skin. "I love you," he gritted out. "Grace, I love you so much. I want to grow old with you. Spend my life learning to love the way I didn't know that I could."

"I love you, too," she replied and then she tilted her hips so the head of his cock slipped inside her warm, soft channel.

He'd begun to shake. Bad wasn't certain when exactly that had happened but now he couldn't control the response.

He inched deeper into her tight sheath, the control he was exercising near breaking him. He felt her maidenhead and he thrust against it, breaking it in one quick movement.

She cried out, pulling him closer and he stilled, his lips brushing her temple, then her nose. "Are you all right, love?"

"I…" she started, tightening her hold. "I am. It just hurt…" She paused again. "More than I expected."

His body cried to move but he held still. "I'm sorry, sweetheart. It only hurts this one time." He kissed her cheeks, her jaw. "The pain will go away soon."

She nodded, pressing her face into the crook of his neck. "When the pain goes away, does it feel as good as your kisses?"

That made him relax. "I believe so." He'd heard more than a few say it was even better but he'd allow her to draw her own conclusions.

She stretched out, relaxing underneath him. "Really? Better?" She lightly stroked his neck. "No wonder women allow themselves to be ruined." Then she giggled. "I have allowed myself to be ruined."

It was his turn to tense. "You're marrying me now, Grace. There's no backing out of it and—"

She tilted back her chin and took a kiss. "I tease." Then another. "Besides, it's fun to be bad. Especially when I know you'll make an honest woman of me."

He drew in a long breath and then rolled onto his back, rolling her with him so that he stayed inside her. "It is fun, but we will be married very shortly."

Being on top, she moved a bit on his staff, making pleasure tighten his sac. "After we're married, can we pretend not to be?"

"What?" He stopped moving, holding her hips. His old fears reared to the surface. "What do you hope to gain by pretending not to be married?"

She moved against him again, her hips pulling him deeper into her body. "You could come to my chamber pretending to be a servant or…" She looked up at the ceiling. "My solicitor."

Dear God, the woman was discussing role play. She really was perfect. "Grace." He pushed the word out through gritted teeth. "I will do whatever you ask if you just move your hips like that again."

"Hmmmm," she answered. "Like this?" And she swirled her hips making pleasure rock through his body.

"Yes," he hissed, holding onto her hips. "Again."

"So bossy," she murmured, slowing the pace further. It only heightened his pleasure. "As your queen, I demand you lay quietly."

A laugh nearly burst from his lips, but he clamped his mouth closed. His sassy woman could say whatever she wanted. "Yes, my love."

And suddenly, she stopped moving slow and began to take him faster and faster, her hands planted on either side of his head, her hair creating a glorious tent about their faces that shut out the rest of the world so it was only them.

He dug his fingers into her soft flesh, helping her to move over him until they were both breathless with desire.

His body was taut as a bowstring as he tingled with the need to release his seed. He held on until she spasmed over him, crying out his name.

Only then did he let his own pleasure go.

They lay there together, wrapped in each other's arms, kissing and murmuring softly until finally Grace lay her head on his chest. He was still inside her and it occurred to him that he had never, in his entire life, been this satisfied, felt so complete.

"Ben," she murmured, her middle finger skimming over his nipple. "Is it always like this?"

"I've never felt this way before," he answered. The words were true but he took extra satisfaction in saying them. "What we have is special."

"I assumed as much," she replied, her voice sleepy. "If every coupling was like this, no one would do anything else."

He choked on a laugh, but her soft sigh of sleep told him she hadn't heard it. His little minx was sound asleep.

CHAPTER SEVENTEEN

Two days later...

Grace stepped off the boat, drinking in the lovely landscape that greeted her. Beyond the village where they'd docked lay craggy cliffs and green fields as far as her eye could see. She drew in a deep breath of the ocean air, so fresh and clean after London.

"Have you ever lived anywhere else besides the city?" she asked Ben, whose hand was firmly about her waist exactly where it was meant to be.

He shook his head. "I haven't. Not that I remember anyway. I've visited the country estate entailed with my lands but didn't stay long."

She nodded. "I always thought I preferred London. More exciting. But standing here…"

He brushed a kiss across her temple like a painter might brush his canvas. "You see the beauty of the landscape, the quiet repose we might have together in such a place."

"Yes." She looked up at him, her eyes sparkling. "How did you know I was going to say that?"

"I was thinking it too," he answered, squeezing her closer. "Two days together and I feel as though…" He paused.

"We grow more connected." Grace picked up his thought.

"Yes," he said, touching his forehead to hers. "After we return to your family, it might be nice to spend the summer away from the crowds. Spend time just being together."

"I agree," she said, love swelling her chest. "Though we should likely marry first."

He smiled. "That we can do. Although…"

For the first time in two days, she felt out of touch with what he was thinking and a bit of fear tingled through her fingertips. "I've left London with you. You're not changing your mind now, are you?"

He straightened, his eyebrows drawing together. "Of course not. How could you even think such a thing?"

She reached for his biceps, holding them in her hands. "My old fears, I suppose."

He gave a nod, dropping his forehead back to hers. "That, I completely understand. But let's leave those in London. I am ready to accept the fact that you might be able to love me if you can accept the fact that you are more, in every way, than I ever dared to wish for."

A soft smile played at her lips. "And to think, you thought you weren't good with words. That was the most beautiful thing I've ever heard."

He chuckled then. "You bring it out in me." Then he gathered her closer. Ben took a step back, and then with his arm about her, walked her down the plank.

"So why did you hesitate when you talked of our wedding?" she asked when they reached the bottom.

"Well…" he started. "I've a surprise for you but I don't know when exactly that surprise will arrive."

"Surprise?" She crinkled her brow. What could he possibly have surprised her with? "Running away to Scotland wasn't adventure enough?"

He stopped walking and then raised his hand, pointing through the crowd of sailors leaving the boat. "There."

She stood on tiptoe, straining through the crowd, but she wasn't nearly as tall as him and couldn't see what he pointed at. The morning sun glinted off the rock causing her to squint as she searched. "Where?"

"Grace?" a female voice called from the crowd. "Grace, is that you?"

Cordelia? "No," she gasped, covering her mouth with her hands. "How is my cousin here?"

Ben winked. "I sent Malice a letter the day before we sailed. I'd hoped you would say yes."

She gave him a sidelong glance. "For a man who was uncertain about my affection, you seemed rather certain about my actions." Then she swatted his arm. "And thank you. This is a wonderful surprise."

He grinned as he began pulling her through the crowd toward her cousin and his friend. When they reached Cordelia, she threw her arms about her, so glad to have her cousin here now. "I'm so happy to see you. How did you get here so quickly?"

Cordelia hugged Grace tight. "We were here already. Getting ready to sail north to see Chad's family."

Grace held Cordelia tight. "How fortunate we didn't miss you."

"How does everything fare down south?" Malice rumbled as he shook Ben's hand. "Did you leave because you weren't safe?"

Grace backed up as she waved her hand. "Ben took care of all that."

Malice raised a brow but didn't say more.

Ben clapped his hand on Malice's shoulder. "We're here because Grace's mother wanted to plan a very elaborate wedding sometime in the distant future and—"

Cordelia let out a tinkling laugh. "Say no more. I know how overbearing my aunt can be." Then she reached for Grace's hand. "I know just where the blacksmith is located. Let's go see him now."

―――

BAD'S HEART raced in his chest. Grace was about to be his, absolutely and completely. His fear was still there, of course. A lifetime of feeling unworthy hadn't washed away in a single night.

But those worries had lessened and with each day by Grace's side—and honestly, each night in her bed—they further washed away. He'd still love her long after her blonde hair had faded to grey and wrinkles spidered out from the corners of her eyes.

She'd love him too, he grew more certain of that every day. Not that he wouldn't work hard to give her what she wanted. He'd do nearly anything to keep her happy.

And right now, that meant marrying her in a blacksmith's shop in a small village in Scotland with the spring sun shining down on them. He grinned as the sun glinted off her hair, her arm linked with Cordelia's, and she tossed a smile at him over her shoulder.

"You look like a man in love," Malice rumbled next to him, his deep voice, carrying despite the fact that he hadn't spoken very loudly.

"I am," he answered simply. Then he turned to his friend. "So do you."

Malice shook his head. "How did it happen? One minute we're happy bachelors, intent upon debauchery and the next…" He waved his hand at the women. "I spend hours a day considering how to make Cordelia happier. I'm helping her to write a book, can you believe that?"

"You're writing a book?" Bad stopped to stare at his friend.

Malice shook his head. "I can't write for a hill of beans. I'm her secretary, recording her words since she injured her hand." Malice ran his hand through his hair. "What's more astounding is that I love the task. To listen to her voice, to see her mind at work." He gave a quiet sigh. "I've completely fallen under her spell."

Bad didn't look at his friend. Instead, he stared at the woman who had bewitched him. "I'd throw myself in the Thames to protect Grace. Hell, I chased her across half of England to save her. Even managed to get myself shot."

Malice laughed. "Not so unusual for you."

Bad quirked a brow. "We're moving to the country."

A laugh burst from Malice's chest. "Well, that is interesting indeed. Love has struck you for certain."

The blacksmith's shop lay just ahead, the sound of his hammer, permeating the quiet street. "I can't wait to make her my wife. I—"

Malice clapped him on the shoulder. "I'm glad I get to stand next to you when you do. No one deserves a happy ending more than you, my friend."

The air whooshed from his lungs as gratitude filled his chest. He was thankful to Malice for being here but also to Daring for suggesting this. It wasn't just Grace who benefitted, but himself. He'd lost his family long ago but he'd gained a new one without realizing it. The men who'd ran the club with him, they'd become his brothers. "I'm glad too. Thank you," he said, then hugged Malice, something he'd never done before in his entire life.

And Malice hugged him back.

The blacksmith was ready within a quarter hour to see their nuptials completed. He tied their hands with ribbon, joining them together as they promised to love and cherish one another for the rest of their days.

As he stared into Grace's eyes, he had the distinct feeling that his love for her would not only be with him in this life but into the next.

EPILOGUE

Two months later...

Grace stood in front of the church looking onto the busy London street as carriages and people passed noisily by. She could see her parents' house from the front steps. In fact, she'd grown up attending this very parish. She snapped her fan open and gave it a wave, cooling her skin from the summer heat. The country was so much more comfortable this time of year.

Her mother twitched next to her. "Did you see the flowers inside? Aren't they marvelous?"

"Of course, mother. With you planning this blessed occasion, how could they be anything but?"

Her mother beamed. "Thank you, dear." Then she turned to her daughter. "Of course, this was supposed to be your wedding."

Grace sniffed as Diana chuckled next to her. "Yes, Grace. You went off and eloped without even inviting me."

Grace reached for her sister's hand. "I'm sorry for that. But Ben and I simply couldn't wait. Other than missing you, I've not a single regret."

"What about me? Didn't you miss having me?" Emily said as she climbed from her carriage. She wore a lovely pale blue empire waist silk and lace gown that mostly hid her growing belly.

"You know I did." She grinned at her eldest sister. "And you look absolutely stunning."

Emily gave a quick curtsy as Minnie stepped out from the carriage behind Emily. Her eyebrows were raised. "Which begs the question. Why did you give up this opportunity? No one likes beautiful gowns and ribbons more than you."

Grace gave a shrug but inside, happiness and love filled her chest. "Some things in life are more important than pretty dresses."

All of the women laughed. "My God, Grace. How you've grown," Diana gave her hand a squeeze. "I'm so happy for you and Lord Baderness."

"Thank you," she whispered. But then she turned to Emily. "But today is about Emily and Lord Effington."

Emily blushed. "It was a rough start but I think we've finally found our way."

Grace covered her heart with her hand. "I'm so glad for both of you. You deserve to have a happy ending."

Emily winked. "And mother deserved the opportunity to plan one wedding."

Mary, their spinster cousin, stepped out of the carriage. She gave a long sigh. "It's moments like these that I wish I'd been able to find someone."

Mary was four and twenty and had never married. A petite blonde, Mary had a delicate beauty and an even kinder heart.

Minnie reached for her hand. "You still could. Both of our fathers would help you." Mary's fiancé had been a soldier who had never returned from the war. Somehow, she'd never been able to move on.

Mary shook her head. "I like working and I'm content with my future." But her eyes held a sadness that belied her words.

"You've gotten a new position now that we don't need a companion?"

Mary nodded. "Darlington found it for me. I'm to be a tutor for the Earl of Sinclair."

Minnie raised a brow and gave Grace a long look. "Have you met the earl yet?"

Mary shook her head. "No. Why? Is there something I should know? Is he old and awful?"

Grace pursed her lips. "Quite the contrary. He's young and extremely handsome."

The women about her shuffled. His nickname was the Earl of Sin.

Mary sniffed. "I am immune to such things."

Her mother gestured for all the women to step forward. "Come. Let's go inside. We've a wedding to begin, after all."

Emily stepped to the front of the group. "My wedding." She gave a sigh. "I'm so glad to have made it to this moment."

Grace gave Emily a peck on the cheek. "We'll go take our seats. I'd wish you luck but you don't need it."

Turning she made her way inside. The moment her eyes adjusted, she caught sight of Ben waiting for her near the front of the church. Rushing to his side, he slipped an arm about her even as he kissed her forehead. "My love."

She gave him a quick squeeze. "I can't wait to see the wedding. It's so exciting."

He held her close, resting his forehead on top of hers. "You are magnificent."

She looked up at her husband. "Me?" His scars were barely visible in this light and his strength radiated through her. "Don't tell anyone, because I mean no offense to my cousins and sisters, but I am the luckiest woman in all of England."

The organ started but she didn't turn back right away, Ben held her to his side. "I love you so very much," he whispered.

"I love you too." She gave him a quick peck on the cheek before she turned to watch Emily float down the aisle toward Jack's outstretched hands. After all the insanity with the club and the Countess of Abernath, the world had righted itself again.

EARL OF SIN

Miss Mary Chase stood at the front gate of the stately mansion situated in the heart of London and stared up at the imposing brick façade. It wasn't too late to turn around, go back to her aunt and uncle's, resume her life.

Lord and Lady Winthrop had taken her in after the loss of her parents seven years ago, even financed a season for her. But she could not, in good conscience, continue to leech off them with no prospect of marriage.

Her aunt insisted she could still find a husband but Mary knew how these things worked. In all likelihood, she'd get passed by. She was four and twenty, after all. No man would want her now. A season would be the exclamation point on the sentence of her life. *You weren't meant for a happily ever after, Mary! Haven't you learned that yet?*

And so instead of another season, she'd accepted an interview for the position of tutor within the home of the Earl of Sinclair.

Her family was mildly appalled. Unlike many girls who'd become orphans, she'd been treated with love and kindness and she'd happily acted as companion to several of her cousins. But she was of age now, and, in her mind, that meant that she ceased to be a burden to them

EARL OF SIN

and learned how to care for herself. Besides, she liked being useful. In a life that had been filled with loss, she found real joy in work.

She straightened her shoulders as she approached the front steps. She'd not lose her resolve now. After fixing the ribbons on her bonnet, she raised her hand and lifted the knocker, giving two decisive smacks to the brass plate on the door.

The sound echoed through the house and her insides quivered along with the noise. But she'd gone too far now to back down, so she held her breath as she waited for the door to open.

When her lungs were near bursting, the door swung in, and a tall butler with an amazingly erect back, stared down at her. "Yes?"

Mary swallowed, pressing her hands together. "I'm here for the position of tutor." The earl's daughter, as she understood it, had lost her mother some time ago and the earl wished for a woman of society to teach his daughter how to properly behave. As a spinster who had grown up in the house of an earl, she was perfect for such a task.

The butler's mouth turned down. "I thought you would enter by the kitchen door." He gave her a long look up and down.

Drat. Her chest tightened. She was no longer a member of the family but a servant. How could she have forgotten that? The look on the butler's face assured her he was wondering the same. She dropped into a quick curtsy. Here, the butler was above her in station. "Of course. My apologies."

He gave her a single nod, his expression unchanged. "His lord is expecting you. Follow me."

Her stomach twisted into an uncomfortable knot and she drew in a deep breath to calm it. Mary would not allow her nerves to get the better of her. She had a multitude of family to rely on should this position fall through. She needn't be worried.

Today felt like the beginning of her new life. One where she was independent and able to care for herself. If she failed, she'd be proving she couldn't even complete the simple task of providing for her own future. If she couldn't do that, what could she do exactly? Of what use was she to this world?

The butler started up the stairs and she followed. She'd expected some sort of introduction. When none came, in her usual fashion, she began it herself. "My name is Mary Chase," she murmured, unsure of what else to say. "It's a pleasure to meet you."

"I know," he answered, not looking back. "Should you succeed in this interview, I shall introduce you to the staff."

She pressed her lips together. Apparently, the man wasn't going to perform the basic nicety of giving his name without first making certain she would stay. She had the distinct impression he didn't like her, but why? He didn't even know her.

They reached the top of the stairs and Mary followed him down a lovely hallway, lined with beautifully polished oak panels and covered in thick carpet that dulled their footsteps until they reached an open door.

The butler stepped inside while she remained in the hall. "Miss Chase is here to see you."

"Send her in," a deep male voice replied.

The sound reverberated through her in the most pleasant way. Both strong and capable, she wanted to sigh just hearing those three short words.

The butler turned back to her and waved her forward, with a flick of his hand.

Straightening her back again, she stepped into the room as the butler moved to the side. But she didn't bother to look at him, instead studying the earl. The first thing she noted was the dark crown of his hair as he bent at the desk, finishing some task with his quill. His hair was a touch overlong, which suited him nicely. Rich brown waves swept back from his forehead and down his neck, nearly brushing the nape of his neck. But his hair was forgotten as she noted the breadth of his shoulders, strength of his arms, and the large capable hands that held the tiny quill.

Then he looked up, smiling at her. Chocolate colored eyes and classically handsome nose and cheeks gave way to a strong jaw and lips...dear Lord, his lips were the most kissable she'd ever encountered. Even more so than her former fiancé Steven's had been. The thought shocked her and parched her throat. Then air rushed from her lungs as his voice echoed through her again.

"Miss Chase, I presume? It's a pleasure to meet you. The Duke of Darlington has spoken very highly of your abilities. My daughter is in desperate need of aid."

Dear Lord, she was in trouble. So very much.

Lord Colbert Sinclair, or Sin as his friends called him, assessed the woman in front of him, noting that she was far prettier than he'd prefer. In fact, she was stunning. Daring hadn't mentioned that fact when he'd suggested Mary as a potential tutor.

He'd expected a woman who was older, matronly. She'd have greying hair, with a few wrinkles about the eyes that gave her a kind look. Perhaps she'd be a bit thick in the middle, which would make her excellent for the sort of hugs small girls needed.

The woman before him now embodied none of these attributes. A petite blonde, she had eyes the color of the sky on a clear, bright summer day and the sort of small features that gave her an air of delicate beauty. The last thing he wished for was a woman of beauty in the house.

His first wife had been beautiful. Petite like Mary, she'd brought out every protective instinct Sin possessed. In fact, Mary's resemblance to Clara was rather alarming. Not in the details, of course, but the build, the hair.

He'd loved his wife dearly and had tried to shield her from this harsh world. That was until he couldn't protect her. His insides clenched as he mentally pushed the feeling aside. He didn't need another woman to keep safe. He'd already failed at that task once with his wife and now he had a daughter who worried him constantly. More so of late.

Besides, she was here for a teaching position, not as a candidate for his hand. And to that end, he'd wanted an elderly matron to love Anne, not a woman who was young enough to be her mother. That was essential. Mary, connected in society and beautiful as she was, would likely only be a temporary figure in their lives. He needed someone stable and constant in Anne's life.

And certainly not a woman so lovely.

"It's a pleasure to meet you as well, my lord," she murmured, dropping into a curtsy. "Thank you for granting me this interview."

He grimaced. Daring had left out some key facts. Likely on purpose. But Mary was here now, he might as well conduct the interview. Anne had been a precocious child up to a few months ago. A mad woman had stolen her from his home and since then, his lovely daughter had grown fearful and had retreated into a shell. Or perhaps, he had grown overprotective and pushed her into one. "It is my pleasure." He gestured toward the chair. "Please. Have a seat." Either way, he needed the right person to draw her out again. There was a kindness in Mary's eyes that suited the position and he was tempted to hire her, but something else held him back. What if Anne grew attached to the woman? Just like him, his daughter had suffered loss. He didn't want to put either of them through that again.

She did as he instructed, her back straight as she stared at a spot on his desk. "Thank you."

"Tell me. Have you ever tutored a young girl before?"

She nodded. "I've lived with my aunt and uncle since I was sixteen. Grace was only nine." Her hands tightened into a knot on her lap. "Not quite as young as your daughter but I can assure you, Grace was a handful."

Sin smiled. "I've met her. I have to agree." He cleared his throat. "And your education?"

Her gaze was still fixed somewhere below his. "I was a student as Lady Kitteridge's School of Comportment. My marks were excellent."

He drew in a long breath. That was excellent news. While he wished for his daughter to regain her confidence, he did not want to sacrifice her future as a lady. Much as he hated to admit it, Mary suited the position well in that regard. "Did you attend a season?"

"One," she answered, her features tightening.

He cocked his head to the side, assessing her. "Why just one?" With

EARL OF SIN

her uncle being an earl, surely she could have had several. Could still decide to rejoin society and find a fitting husband.

"I was engaged to the second son of the Earl of Everly, but he was lost in the Napoleonic Wars four years ago."

He gripped his quill harder. Bloody hell that was rough. Almost as terrible as his own story. "I'm sorry for your loss. You didn't see fit to reenter society?"

She shook her head. "No, my lord."

"And you're leaving your aunt and uncle's house because?"

Her eyes rose to his then. They crinkled at the corners in a bit of sadness. He understood it completely. His stomach tightened in understanding and, if he were honest, attraction. Not a feeling he welcomed. "My cousins have all married and no longer need a companion. I can't justify being a dependent in my uncle's house if I am not serving a purpose there."

He straightened, appreciation making his chin tuck back. "Surely, he would continue to support you."

Her delicate shoulders rose then fell. The curve of them was lovely and his fingers itched to trace their slender shape. "I'm sure he would. But I will not be a burden to my family any more than I've already been. I'm perfectly capable of working."

He blinked. He had to confess, for her small stature she was decidedly determined. He liked that. Honestly, he liked her.

Which was dangerous. She'd be his employee, which meant he needed to remain detached from her. Besides, she looked strikingly like his first wife and that was the type of woman he'd never touch again.

Want to read more? Earl of Sin

Keep up with all the latest news, sales, freebies, and releases by joining my newsletter!

www.tammyandresen.com

Hugs!

OTHER TITLES BY TAMMY

The Dark Duke's Legacy

Her Wicked White

Her Wanton White

His Wallflower White

Her Willful White

Her Wanton White

His White Wager

Her White Wedding

Lords of Scandal

Duke of Daring

Marquess of Malice

Earl of Exile

Viscount of Vice

Baron of Bad

Earl of Sin

Earl of Gold

Earl of Baxter

Duke of Decandence

Marquess of Menace

Duke of Dishonor

Baron of Blasphemy

Viscount of Vanity

Earl of Infamy

Laird of Longing

The Dark Duke's Legacy

Her Wicked White

Her Willful White

His Wallflower White

Her Wanton White

Her Wild White

His White Wager

Her White Wedding

The Rake's Ruin

When only an Indecent Duke Will Do

How to Catch an Elusive Earl

Where to Woo a Bawdy Baron

When a Marauding Marquess is Best

What a Vulgar Viscount Needs

Who Wants a Brawling Baron

When to Dare a Dishonorable Duke

The Wicked Wallflowers

Earl of Dryden

Too Wicked to Woo

Too Wicked to Wed

Too Wicked to Want

How to Reform a Rake

Don't Tell a Duke You Love Him

Meddle in a Marquess's Affairs

Never Trust an Errant Earl

Never Kiss an Earl at Midnight

Make a Viscount Beg

Wicked Lords of London

Earl of Sussex

My Duke's Seduction

My Duke's Deception

My Earl's Entrapment

My Duke's Desire

My Wicked Earl

Brethren of Stone

The Duke's Scottish Lass

Scottish Devil

Wicked Laird

Kilted Sin

Rogue Scot

The Fate of a Highland Rake

A Laird to Love

Christmastide with my Captain

My Enemy, My Earl

Heart of a Highlander

A Scot's Surrender

A Laird's Seduction

Taming the Duke's Heart

Taming a Duke's Reckless Heart

Taming a Duke's Wild Rose

Taming a Laird's Wild Lady

Taming a Rake into a Lord

Taming a Savage Gentleman

Taming a Rogue Earl

Fairfield Fairy Tales

Stealing a Lady's Heart

Hunting for a Lady's Heart

Entrapping a Lord's Love: Coming in February of 2018

American Historical Romance

Lily in Bloom

Midnight Magic

The Golden Rules of Love

Boxsets!!

Taming the Duke's Heart Books 1-3

American Brides

A Laird to Love

Wicked Lords of London

ABOUT THE AUTHOR

Tammy Andresen lives with her husband and three children just outside of Boston, Massachusetts. She grew up on the Seacoast of Maine, where she spent countless days dreaming up stories in blueberry fields and among the scrub pines that line the coast. Her mother loved to spin a yarn and Tammy filled many hours listening to her mother retell the classics. It was inevitable that at the age of eighteen, she headed off to Simmons College, where she studied English literature and education. She never left Massachusetts but some of her heart still resides in Maine and her family visits often.

Find out more about Tammy:
http://www.tammyandresen.com/
https://www.facebook.com/authortammyandresen
https://twitter.com/TammyAndresen
https://www.pinterest.com/tammy_andresen/
https://plus.google.com/+TammyAndresen/

Printed in Great Britain
by Amazon